Kelly's Koffee Shop

A Cedar Bay Cozy Mystery

DIANNE HARMAN

Gloucester Library
P.O. Box 2380
Gloucester, VA 23061

Published by: Dianne Harman
www.dianneharman.com

Interior, cover design and website by
Vivek Rajan Vivek
www.vivekrajanvivek.com

ISBN: 978-1503015630

CONTENTS

ACKNOWLEDGMENTS

As always, I could not have written this without the help of my husband, Tom. He has become a master chef and gardener, as well as king of the laundry! Thank you!

To Rhys, Pamela, Kay, Deanna, Charlene, Kathleen, Janice, Christoph, Dave and Jeanie, and all the rest of you who so willingly helped me and gave me feedback, thank you! A book becomes a living thing, and all of your input definitely made it healthier.

And to all of you who have read my books and taken the time to contact me and give me your input, please know how very much it's appreciated. Readers, none of this would be possible without you. Thank you!

CHAPTER ONE

The fading moonlight cast a warm glow on the quiet waters of Cedar Bay as Kelly and her big boxer, Rebel, drove the six blocks from her home to Kelly's Koffee Shop located at the end of the pier that jutted out into the bay. At this early hour of the morning, the only traffic was the occasional logging truck that rumbled through town. Cedar Bay was quite small and only had one stop light, at the intersection of Main and Cedar. The city fathers had installed it many years ago to keep the logging trucks from speeding through town.

Lush cedar forests surrounded the town, named after the lumber industry that had given birth to it. When the town was first built on the central Oregon coast, ships anchored in the small harbor, and then transported the lumber to its final destination. Even when the large ships were replaced by the railroads and logging trucks and the harbor was converted into a small marina for recreational boats, the loggers still came to Kelly's Koffee Shop whenever they wanted a good, home-cooked breakfast or lunch.

Kelly pulled into the harbor parking lot next to the pier and noticed that Amber's car wasn't in its usual place and there was no sign of her. She was usually standing at the door, waiting for Kelly to open up. *Wonder what that's all about*, she thought.

"Amber, are you here?" she asked in a loud voice as she opened the door and turned on the lights. Kelly had given her an emergency key, but Amber was to use it only for that purpose. She wondered if Amber had gone into the coffee shop even though no lights were on when Kelly had pulled into the parking lot. Her question was met by an eerie silence. There was no answer from Amber.

Swell, this is not a good way to start the day. This is a first. Wonder why she's not here.

She plugged in the big commercial coffeepot and turned on the ovens, knowing that within an hour, the popular coffee shop she owned would be filled with hungry and thirsty regulars. Kelly knew nearly every shop owner and citizen in the little town and knew that many of them would be starting their mornings or having lunch at the coffee shop in the coming week. A few minutes later, Roxie, the longtime waitress at Kelly's, came through the front door, followed by Charlie, the short-order cook.

"Roxie, did Amber mention anything to you about not coming in this morning?"

"No. I said goodbye to her yesterday afternoon after we finished cleaning up, just like I do every day," the blond blue-eyed waitress said. Kelly had come to rely on Roxie, who had been with her for over ten years. Roxie never forgot a customer's name, really cared about what was going on in each of their lives, and while she didn't have the looks of a movie star, her welcoming smile and friendly blue eyes made her just as attractive to the customers of Kelly's Koffee Shop, particularly the male customers.

Kelly and Roxie were like Mutt and Jeff. In contrast to Roxie, who at 5'3" was rather short, Kelly was tall with jet black hair she wore pulled back either in a ponytail or twisted and secured at the back of her head with a large tortoiseshell clip. Intelligent sea-green eyes never seemed to miss anything that was going on at the coffee shop, or for that matter, anywhere else. It was a casual seaside town and Kelly's signature uniform was jeans and a red T-shirt, covered with a white apron with the words "Kelly's Koffee Shop" embroidered on it in large red letters.

"Well, maybe she overslept," Kelly said, "although that sure isn't like her. Glad you and Amber set the tables before you left yesterday."

Promptly at 7:00 a.m. the first customer opened the door. "Morning, Rebel, morning, Kelly," the big burly county sheriff said, bending down and scratching Rebel's ears. The more he scratched, the faster Rebel's tail wagged. "What's the special breakfast casserole today?" He was in his standard uniform which consisted of a grey shirt, loden green pants, white Stetson hat, and his gun in its holster on his hip. His hairline was receding and there were a few extra pounds on his 6'3" frame, but he carried himself with an air of authority. You only had to take one look at the man to know this was someone you didn't want to cross.

"Sausage and eggs, Mike, plus I've got some sweet rolls about ready to come out of the oven," she said smiling at him as she poured his coffee.

"I swear Kelly, no woman should look as good as you do this early in the morning. What's your secret?"

"Wish I had one, but I don't. Mike, I'm a little concerned about Amber, She didn't show up this morning and she's never been late before."

"With graduation coming up next week, she's probably playing hooky. I wouldn't worry. She's a good kid. Pretty impressive that she and Brandon, two of the town's own, are going to Oregon State in the fall on full scholarships. As tight as money is for Amber's parents, she probably couldn't have gone to college without the scholarship. Course Brandon's family doesn't need to worry about it. His parents could pay for him to go anywhere he wants. Do you think they'll continue seeing each other after they've settled into college life?"

"Who knows? Been my experience not many high school sweethearts stay together once they get to college."

"Speaking of romance, what are the chances of me coming by for dinner tonight?" Mike asked with a twinkle in his eye.

"Pretty good. Say about seven?"

"See you then. I know, no more talking. You need to get to get to work." He looked at the large piece of the breakfast casserole and the sweet roll Roxie placed in front of him. "Thanks, Roxie. Looks great!"

"Wish I could say it was my recipe, but it's from Kelly's mom. It's one of our customers' favorites."

Mike cut a piece off of the large swirled cinnamon and glazed sweet roll and put it in his mouth. He turned his eyes up and made a swooning gesture and said out of the side of his mouth, "I think I've died and gone to heaven."

"Oh you! I know it's good, Mike, but I think you may be overdoing it," Roxie said, playfully swatting his shoulder.

"Trust me, this is manna from heaven. If starting out the day with this sweet roll is any indication, then it's going to be a very good day." Later that evening, he remembered those lighthearted words because it turned out it would be a day the citizens of Cedar Bay would long remember, a day that turned out not to be a very good day.

Rebel, Kelly's big boxer, was in his favorite spot in the coffee shop, lying on his dog bed next to the front door, not far from the cash register. Every time someone opened the door, he acknowledged them by looking up and hoping they'd scratch his ears for a couple of minutes. A number of them did just that before they sat down at the counter or at one of the tables. Rebel was a gentle giant, but the regulars knew he felt his one purpose in life was to protect Kelly at all times. If she went in the kitchen, he did too. She was never out of his sight.

"Roxie, I'll have the usual," the handsome suntanned man said as he walked in and sat down at the counter after first stopping to greet

Rebel. He gave the room a once-over. "You know, every morning when I come here I look around at all the old photos on the walls of how the town looked years ago. There's everything from photos of the mule teams dragging logs to the harbor, to lumberjacks using huge handsaws to fell the old growth cedar trees, to the Native Americans who lived here before Cedar Bay was built. It's kind of like a glimpse into the past of this area. I seem to always find something in the photos I hadn't noticed before."

"Yeah, I know what you mean. Kelly's grandparents were some of the original settlers here. You can see how the town grew just by lookin' at the photos," Roxie said as she poured his coffee.

Chris Jones was a fairly recent arrival in Cedar Bay. From what the townspeople knew, he'd come to Cedar Bay a year ago from Idaho, smarting from a bitter divorce. The local high school hired him as its English teacher and football coach. The Cedar Bay football team won its first conference title in eighteen years under his guidance. He was something of a loner and although he preferred to keep to himself and spend time living alone on his boat which he kept docked in the marina, he was a hero to the townspeople.

Even though Cedar Bay was a small town of only a few thousand people, and it was a month before tourist season would be in full swing, Kelly's Koffee Shop was doing its usual good business. It had become something of an institution in the small town. The coffee shop had been part of Kelly's life from the time she was born. Her grandmother had baked pies that she and Kelly's grandfather sold out of a small building on the pier. Most of their customers were the loggers who worked in the timber industry. Over time, as the business grew and as her customers began to ask for other kinds of food, the small shop had expanded several times. When Kelly's parents had taken over the coffee shop, they named it Kelly's Koffee Shop in honor of their daughter. They'd retired many years ago and moved to a seniors' community near Phoenix.

It was a given that Kelly and her husband would run the coffee shop when her parents retired. A few years later when Mark, Kelly's husband, died unexpectedly at an early age from a rare type of bone cancer, the coffee shop provided the money Kelly needed to raise their children and also gave her a reason to get up in the morning. No one expects their husband to die when he's just thirty-one years old. It hadn't been easy, but she'd managed to be both a mother and father to her daughter and son. Julia lived in San Francisco and worked for a large bank in their loan department. She usually came to see Kelly at least once a month. Kelly's son, Cash, was a career Marine presently stationed in the Middle East, but he too, made it home as often as he could. It had only been recently that Kelly had made room in her life for Mike, the county sheriff. The children were gone, she was lonesome, and he was a good man. A lot of relationships started with less.

The morning flew by with regulars and a few tourists, all hungry and thirsty. The popular coffee shop was only open for breakfast and lunch. If you wanted to eat at Kelly's, you often had to wait for a seat.

Like clockwork, promptly at noon the door opened and Doc walked in, pausing for a moment to scratch Rebel's ears. "Hi Kelly, what's the special today?"

"We just ran out of the breakfast special, but I've got that barbecued brisket you like. Got some great au gratin potatoes and a mini-monkey bread to go with it. How does that sound?"

"Great. I'd also like a tall iced tea. It's starting to get warm. We may be in for a long summer. Where's Amber? I didn't see her when I pulled up. She and I usually come in at the same time now that she doesn't have cheerleading practice after class."

"Don't know. She didn't come in this morning. I've been meaning to call Ginger and ask her if Amber's sick, but it's been so busy I haven't had a chance. I'll call in a few minutes. How are things out on the ranch?"

Doc lived about five minutes outside of town in an old ranch house surrounded by ten acres. Ever since he'd come to Cedar Bay, he'd been a mystery to the townspeople. No one knew anything about him other than that his nickname was Doc. Like a few other people in the area, Doc apparently wanted to "live off the grid." All Kelly or anyone else knew about him were his food choices. He didn't even bank at the First Federal, Cedar Bay's only bank. Grizzled and deeply tanned, the only time anyone ever saw him was during the week at noon at Kelly's Koffee Shop. Kelly's was closed on Saturdays and Sundays and there was some speculation among the town gossips about what Doc did for lunch on the weekends.

Kelly looked up as the door opened. "Hi, Mike. To what do I owe the pleasure of a second visit on the same day?" she asked, laughing.

Mike had a serious look on his weathered face. He looked every day of his fifty-four years. "Have you called Ginger yet? I checked with Suzie over at the high school and Amber wasn't in class today. Brandon was in school so it doesn't look like they decided to take a ditch day. Did a little asking around and no one's seen her all day."

"I'll call Ginger right now," she said, picking up the phone.

"Hi, Ginger, it's Kelly. Wondering if everything's okay with Amber." She paused. "No, she never came to work today. Mike checked with Suzie over at the school and she wasn't in her classes." She listened. "She left earlier than usual and said she wanted to get here and do some studying for a final exam? Well, don't worry; I'm sure it's nothing. She'll probably come in soon and help me close up and get ready for tomorrow. I'll call you if I find out anything. If you hear from her, I'd appreciate it if you'd call me."

She turned to Mike. "I didn't want to frighten her, but now I'm really worried. Ginger and Bob have enough to worry about just making ends meet between the bookstore Ginger owns losing its customers to the Internet and Bob's handyman jobs, which are few and far between. I'm probably his best customer, but there's only so much business I can give him."

"I'll go out to Brandon's place this afternoon and talk to his parents and him. If anyone knows where she is, it would be Brandon. See you at seven." Mike tipped his hat and walked out the door.

CHAPTER TWO

Promptly at 7:00 Kelly heard two knocks on her door. Even though the town was small and everyone knew everyone else's business, Kelly kept her door locked and always looked through the peephole to see who was there before she opened the door. One thing Kelly had learned over the years was that towns near the ocean seemed to attract drifters and people hoping to lose themselves. It hadn't helped the small Oregon town when a number of states legalized marijuana. It was rumored that several local farms and ranches looked like they were growing the usual types of farm products or running cattle, but they were actually fronts for profitable marijuana farms.

The owners planted rows of legal crops to make it look legitimate, but the rows of plants hid the main crop, marijuana. Cattle ranchers used their remote pastures to grow marijuana behind locked gates. Mike had made several arrests over the last few years, but there were several farmers and ranchers that proved to be elusive. Mike had always suspected Brandon Black's father, but he'd never been able to prove it.

Mike knew where Kelly kept the emergency key in the planter on her front porch. He knew of her fear of drifters, so when he used it he always knocked twice, to let her know it was him. "Mike, I'm so glad to see you. Any word on Amber?" Kelly asked as they walked out to the deck that overlooked the bay. "Before you answer, you look like you could use a glass of wine. Pinot okay with you?"

"I could definitely use a glass and yes, a nice Oregon pinot would be great."

"Make yourself comfortable, I'll be back in a minute." He smiled to himself as she walked into the kitchen, thinking what a good looking woman she was even if she was in her early 50's. She had a beautiful smooth white porcelain like complexion which she'd been wise enough to keep out of the sun over the years. A couple of extra pounds spoke to her love of cooking, but didn't detract from her voluptuous figure.

Anyway, that suited Mike just fine. He had never been a fan of skinny women. His ex-wife had been thin and hungry, hungry for the things a county sheriff could never give a woman. She'd found a wealthy doctor when she'd gone to Las Vegas for a "girls' trip." Later Mike discovered that she'd found the wealthy doctor on the Internet well before she'd gone to Las Vegas and there had been no "girls' trip." When she returned from Las Vegas, she filed for divorce. Mike felt if there was a silver lining in their failed marriage, it was that they had never had children.

"I haven't heard anything about Amber. Has Ginger called? Any word from her?" he asked. As county sheriff, it was his job to protect the citizens of the county and a missing young woman was always a cause for concern.

"No. It's as if Amber disappeared into thin air. Just like I told you earlier, Ginger saw her this morning when she left the house and that was the last time anyone has seen her. I'm really worried. Did Brandon know anything?"

"No, and I believe him. He was really distraught and I don't think he was faking it. I talked to his parents, Jeff and Marcy. They said the last time they'd seen Amber was a couple of days ago when she joined them for dinner at the ranch. I've told you before I don't have a good feeling about Brandon's dad. They may be running cattle on that ranch, but I can't shake the feeling he may be doing something more. Looks like Marcy's got a big new diamond ring, at least I've never seen it before. That thing must be three carats. You've got to sell a lot of cattle to afford something like that, more than I think Jeff has. His place is fenced with barbed wire and I would swear I saw a couple of guys with guns on their hips towards the back of the property, but I don't have a valid reason to search it. I'm not even sure Brandon would know if something was going on back there. At that age, kids seem to be pretty oblivious to everything with the exception of what's directly affecting them."

"Well, what do you plan to do now?"

"If Amber doesn't show up tonight, I'm going to go see Ginger and Bob in the morning and get a list of all her friends and relatives and then start making some calls. Someone must know something. It's as if she's completely vanished."

"You might want to start with Madison Riley. I know she's been Amber's nemesis for a long time. Amber told me once that Brandon stopped seeing Madison so he could be with Amber. Evidently she also resented Amber being the head cheerleader and homecoming queen. I don't know if that will help, but…"

"I'll talk to her after I see Ginger. To change the subject, what's for dinner tonight?"

"Well, since you didn't eat lunch at the coffee shop, I thought you'd enjoy the brisket, potatoes, and mini monkey bread. I made a salad from the garden and there's some leftover cheesecake. That should hold you."

He stood up and walked over to her. "Kelly, I know you think I like you just for what you cook…"

Mike was interrupted by his ringing cell phone. "Sorry, I better pick up that call." He listened for a few minutes and grimly told the person on the other end that he'd be there momentarily. He pushed end on the phone and turned to Kelly.

"Kelly, that was Rick who works the night shift at the gas dock down at the marina. A man was fishing from shore and snagged something heavy on his line. It was so heavy he was afraid he'd break his rod, so he kept backing up until he brought it onshore. It was Amber. She was dead. Her body was tied to a burlap bag that had weights in it. He said it looked like she was murdered. From what he told me, I'd have to agree. I think you better go over to Ginger and Bob's and tell them. They shouldn't hear it from someone on the phone."

"Oh no! I can't believe it. You're right. It'll be all over town in minutes. I'll go there right now."

"I've got to get down to the dock. Poor kid. I'll call you later." Mike grabbed the white Stetson hat he always wore and turned to Rebel who sensed something was wrong. He let out a low growl. "Hold the fort, boy. Everything's going to be okay."

CHAPTER THREE

Kelly rang the doorbell on the old, dilapidated house which was badly in need of a paint job. Bob was a handyman and could have easily fixed the sagging porch and replaced the broken shutters, but there wasn't any extra money for the needed materials. Bob and Ginger Cook lived a hand-to-mouth existence and were thrilled when they learned Amber had been accepted at Oregon State and awarded a scholastic scholarship. She was her parents' pride and joy. They knew it was a chance for her to have a much better life than they had led.

Bob answered the door. He took one look at Kelly's face and knew something had happened to Amber. "Have you found something out about Amber?" He turned and yelled down the hall. "Ginger, Kelly's here."

Seconds later a short red-haired freckle faced woman joined them. "Kelly, what is it? What's happened to Amber?"

Kelly put her arms around her best friend and the mother of her godchild. "Ginger, I'm so sorry to have to be the one to tell you this. Amber's body was just brought up on shore. A fisherman thought there was something uncommonly heavy on his line and discovered Amber. Evidently she drowned and before you hear it from other people, I need to tell you that the man who called Mike said it looks like she was murdered. Mike's at the scene right now."

Ginger began screaming and crying at the same time. "No, no, no, not Amber! What did she ever do to deserve this?" Bob put his arms around Ginger who was shaking and led her to the couch. Tears were streaming down both of their faces.

"I'm going to call Dr. Amherst," Kelly said, "and see if he has something he can give me for both of you." She quickly punched in some numbers. "Doctor, it's Kelly Conner. I'm sorry to bother you, but something terrible has happened."

"Yes, Kelly. I just heard about Amber from Mike. I'm on my way to the dock right now. What do you need?"

"I just told Ginger and Bob about Amber. Any chance you could swing by their house and give them something to help them get through the next few hours?"

"Yes, I'll be there in a couple of minutes. Why don't you meet me in their driveway? Mike wants me down at the dock immediately."

"Thanks. See you in a few minutes."

She walked outside and within a few short moments saw Dr. Amherst's old red truck turning the corner. He rolled down the window and handed her a plastic drug bottle. "They can take one of these pills every four hours. It won't bring Amber back, but it might help them make it through the next couple of days."

"I'll make sure they take them. Ginger's sister lives up in Sunset Bay. I'll give her a call and see if she can come over here and stay with them. Remind Mike to give me a call when he knows something."

Several neighbors came to the Cook house as soon as they heard the news about Amber and offered to stay with them until Ginger's sister arrived. Kelly gave the bottle of pills to Ginger and Bob, thanked the neighbors and left, telling them she needed to make some calls. She drove the few blocks to her house, mentally planning who she needed to call. The first call she made was to the high school principal who said he would hold a meeting at the high school first thing in the morning to tell the students and faculty.

Next on her list was the editor of the town newspaper. He'd already had a call from someone who had seen the body brought up. "Kelly, I'll write a eulogy to Amber as well as a story about her death. Based on the call I got, I'm calling it a murder, but of course there's also the possibility that it's a suicide or an accidental drowning. I know she worked for you. Any hint she was having problems?"

"None. You know as much as I do. If she was having problems, I sure wasn't aware of them. It looked like she was headed for a far better life than Ginger and Bob have had. Oh gosh, I just realized no one has probably told Brandon. I better go out there and tell him before someone calls him. If you find out anything, let me know."

She drove as fast as it was safe to the Black's ranch. The large house was situated on a cliff overlooking the ocean accessible only by the long driveway that led up to it from the road. Kelly heard the roar of the surf as soon as she opened the minivan door. *This has got to be the most beautiful location in the world for a house*, she thought, *but if I lived here I'd do something about that smell.* She knocked on the front door of the sprawling ranch house and was greeted by Brandon's father, Jeff Black. "Well, Kelly, I'm hoping you're here because you're bringing me some sweet rolls to go with my morning coffee, but somehow I doubt that's the reason for your trip out here. What's up?"

"Jeff, is Brandon here?"

"Yes. What's the problem? He's in his room studying for a final exam he has tomorrow. Want me to call him?"

"Please, and while you're at it, better ask Marcy to come as well."

He was back in moments with Marcy and Brandon, all of them wondering why Kelly was there. Each of their faces showed concern.

"I'm really sorry to have to be the one to tell you this Brandon, but Amber's body was recovered from the bay a couple of hours ago.

14

It looks like she drowned." She took a deep breath and continued, "Brandon, the man who called Mike and told him about it said it looked like she'd been murdered. Mike and Dr. Amherst are at the scene. Evidently she was discovered by a fisherman."

Everyone in the small town knew that Marcy Black liked to spend money and some said that her husband, Jeff, was pompous and thought he was far better than the other citizens of the small town, but it was very evident to Kelly that Brandon was the number one priority for his parents that night. Tears streamed silently down Brandon's face, as his parents sat beside him on the couch, showing their support for him even though they knew there wasn't much they could do. It was something he would have to go through by himself.

"Are you sure it was her?" Brandon asked. "Who identified her? Maybe it was someone who just looked like her."

"No, Brandon, there were several people on the dock who knew her. I'm sure Mike will be out to talk to you about it, but I didn't want you to hear about it over the phone."

"Kelly, thanks for coming. I know this must have been hard for you. I'll walk you out to your car," Jeff said.

"You're right, this is not the kind of news anyone wants to deliver."

When they got to her minivan, Jeff opened the door for her and asked, "Do you know if she left a note? Could it have been suicide? Do you really think she was murdered? Had she said anything recently about the ranch?"

"Not to my knowledge. I'm sure Mike will discover things, but I've told you everything I know as of this moment. Again, I'm sorry. Death is hard for anyone to accept, particularly when you're eighteen and you think you're invincible. I feel so sorry for Brandon."

"Yeah, this is not going to be easy. I'll wait to hear from Mike. Thanks for driving out here and telling us."

Something about the conversation with Jeff niggled at Kelly as she drove home. *Why would he want to know if Amber had said anything about the Black's ranch? Did Amber know something about it? That's really a strange thing for him to say.*

When she got home, she remembered she needed to call Roxie and ask her to come in a few minutes early the next morning to help her open up the coffee shop. She also made a mental note that she needed to hire someone to replace Amber.

CHAPTER FOUR

Early the next morning, after a long night of tossing and turning, Kelly sleepily rolled out of bed and turned off the alarm clock before it began its shrill ring. Her cell phone rang a moment later. She looked at the screen and saw it was Mike.

"Good morning, Mike. Waited for you to call and then decided I had to get some sleep. What happened last night? Did you find out anything?"

"Sorry. By the time I finished, it was too late to call. It looks like Amber was murdered. Her body was tied to a burlap bag filled with heavy weights like the kind people use when they're working out at home or at the gym. From what Dr. Amherst found in his preliminary investigation, the cause of the death was drowning. She had a large contusion on her head, so he thinks she was hit with some type of blunt instrument and was unconscious when she went into the water."

"Oh, Mike, that's horrible. Why would anyone want to kill her? I feel so sorry for Ginger and Bob. Anything else?"

"Not really. I talked to a lot of people, but no one knows anything about it. Dr. Amherst said he thinks she was probably murdered early yesterday morning and that would fit in with what Ginger told you about her leaving home early. I just can't come up with a motive.

From what I know about Amber, everyone liked her. She was popular, the head cheerleader, homecoming queen, and an outstanding student. I never heard anything negative about her. Do you know of anything?"

"No, I've never heard a bad word about her. Other than what I told you about Madison, I don't think she had an enemy in the world. After I left Ginger and Bob last night, I called a few people, then I went out to the Black's ranch to tell Brandon. I decided that wasn't the kind of news he needed to get over the phone."

"I'm glad you did. How did he take it? Hate to say this, but he could be a person of interest in the case. I'm going out to the ranch first thing today to talk to him."

"Mike, I can't believe Brandon had anything to do with such a terrible crime. He was clearly devastated. Say whatever else you will about Marcy and Jeff, but they were really there for him. Poor kid. What a wake-up call to the real world."

"Well, you better dress and get ready to open the coffee shop. We both know half the people who live in Cedar Bay will probably come to the coffee shop this morning, hoping to hear a fresh tidbit of gossip."

"Wait a second, Mike. Something about the conversation I had with Brandon's dad bothers me. He asked me if Amber left a note or said anything to anyone recently about the ranch. What do you think that was all about?"

He was quiet for a moment. "Well, you know I've always been suspicious of what the main money-making business of the ranch is, but I can't believe Jeff would be involved in something like this. It's pretty clear from Marcy's jewelry and how she dresses that she likes the good life, but I just don't see him doing something that would hurt Brandon. Then again, you never know. Money's a powerful motive for a lot of things. I should know more later on today.

"The county coroner's a good friend of mine and he agreed to perform an autopsy on Amber this afternoon. Usually it takes the coroner's office days, if not weeks, to file an autopsy report. Think my friendship with him helped speed up the process. I'll let you know if I find out anything. See you later."

Kelly and Roxie arrived at the coffee shop at the same time. "Roxie, get the coffee going and put a couple of those breakfast casseroles in the ovens once they warm up. I have a feeling we're going to be jammed today. Matter of fact, think I'll bake a couple of batches of bacon chocolate chip cookies. Most people can't resist chocolate or bacon. Might help to keep the hungry locals at bay. I know it will help calm me down. I'm so sad about this whole thing, it's all I can do to keep from crying," Kelly said, chewing on her lower lip.

The morning flew by as Roxie and Kelly struggled to keep up with the orders. Charlie, the short order cook, never even had a chance to step out for his morning cigarette. He cooked one order after another as Kelly and Roxie brought them to him. It seemed like everyone in the small town stopped by Kelly's Koffee Shop that morning, hoping to get a fresh crumb of gossip. Kelly called Ginger about 11:00. Her sister answered the phone.

"I'm just calling to see how Ginger and Bob are doing. I haven't heard anything more and was wondering if you knew something."

"No. None of us slept last night. Both Ginger and Bob are in shock. I'm going to stay with them for a couple of days. Father Brown's coming by this afternoon to help them make arrangements for the funeral. Ginger remembered that Amber used to keep a diary, but she couldn't find it. She hoped maybe there was something in it that would give us a clue as to why this happened. She doesn't remember Amber mentioning it lately and thinks Amber may have outgrown it and thrown it away. The three of us searched her room for something that might help us figure this out, but we couldn't find anything."

"Well, tell them I called and I'm thinking of them. Also tell them the coffee shop has been jammed with people concerned about them and talking about the tragedy. I just want them to know they're very much loved by everyone in this town. It won't take away the pain they're going through, but maybe it will help a little."

"Thanks, Kelly. I'll give them the message."

Kelly felt a tap on her shoulder and turned around. It was Doc.

"Is it true what everyone's saying – that Amber was murdered? I don't have a television out at the ranch and I just heard about it when I walked in. What do you know about it? I really liked that young woman. Always thought she had a bright future. She and I talked a few times. You know I was a doctor before I retired and I saw a lot of people over the years – good and bad – she was a good one."

"Yes, I agree. She was a good one." She told him the limited information she knew.

When he finished eating, he walked over to the cash register where Kelly was standing. "Kelly, I don't give my phone number out very often, but I'd appreciate it if you'd give me a call when you hear something. Don't know if there's anything I can do, but if I can, I'd be happy to help."

"Thanks, Doc. I'll call you if I hear anything," she said, slipping the piece of paper into her pocket. She watched him as he got in his old battered grey pickup, thinking that was very strange. He'd been coming to Kelly's Koffee Shop for three years and had never become close to anyone, and as far as Kelly knew, he had no friends in the town at all, yet he mentioned he'd talked to Amber several times.

Now what could that be all about? I wonder how he and Amber became friends. What could they possibly have in common? An old grizzled guy trying to live off the grid and a bright young schoolgirl with the rest of her life ahead of her. It makes no sense at all and it's just too strange. I better tell Mike about it.

As Kelly was walking into the kitchen with another order for Charlie, Roxie motioned to her from the storeroom. "Kelly, I'm sorry," she whispered, "but would you serve this to Chief Many

Trees? I swear, that Indian is the surliest, nastiest person who comes in here. Usually I can take his son Charlie talking about their sacred tribal grounds while he's cooking the short orders back in the kitchen, but today I'm having a real problem with both of them. I know it's me, but I just can't deal with the Chief right now. This may be the hardest I've ever worked. Anyway, you're much more tolerant than I am. Here's his order."

Kelly walked through the swinging kitchen doors with the Chief's order of ham, scrambled eggs, and toast. "Good morning, Chief. Saw your order when I went back to the kitchen and didn't want you to wait. As you can see, we're pretty busy this morning."

She set the plate in front of the large Indian who wore his long black hair tied at the back of his neck. Every time she saw the chief, he always had on a large turquoise ring, a turquoise link bracelet set in silver, and a bolo tie with silver points. This morning was no exception.

"Hope it didn't get cold. There's no excuse for cold food, even if you are busy. What's the occasion?" he asked, taking a bite of the eggs.

"It's a sad occasion, Chief. Looks like Amber Cook was murdered. Her body was discovered last night. She drowned."

He paused and looked up at Kelly. "Isn't she the cheerleader that goes with Jeff Black's kid?"

"Yes. She goes with him or I should say, did go with him. Why do you ask?"

"Oh it's probably nothing. I remember hearing something about Black being interested in building some fancy spa near our reservation. His ranch is immediately adjacent to our tribal land and we sure don't want some fancy Las Vegas style hotel and spa that close to it. I'm sure it was just a rumor. Sorry to hear about her."

"Chief, I've got to go. I'd love to stay and talk to you, but I don't want the other diners to have cold food. See you."

When the lunch hour ended and everyone had finally cleared out of the coffee shop, Roxie and Kelly made the final preparations for the next day. The coffee was ready, sweet rolls on cookie sheets were resting in the refrigerator and the overnight casseroles that were such a hit had been made and were ready to be baked the following morning. Kelly had just unplugged the "Open" sign and was getting ready to lock up when the front door opened.

She looked up and was surprised to see Madison standing there. "Madison, come in. I can't give you anything to eat. It's all been put away, but is there something else I can do for you?"

"Yes," she said stepping hesitantly into the room. "I heard about Amber and know she worked for you before and after school. I thought you might be lookin' to hire someone else and I need a job. I'd like to go to cosmetology school in the fall, but Dad says we don't have no money for that. He told me I had to get a job when I graduated from high school and help him with the money. He used to make out okay from fishin', but with all the recent weather changes, he's not catchin' much these days. Only thing he's caught lately was Amber."

"He's the one who brought her up on shore? I didn't know that. I knew a fisherman had found her, but I didn't know it was your dad. I'm sorry. That must have been horrible for him."

"It might have been for him, but not for me. She wasn't a friend of mine. Matter of fact she took my boyfriend away. She beat me out of bein' head cheerleader and then she got the votes to be homecomin' queen. No we weren't close at all. Anyway, the sheriff questioned Dad until late last night, but he don't know nuthin'. He was just fishin' in the bay, like he usually does at dusk, when he snagged her. It was getting dark and his boat ain't as seaworthy as it once was, so he shore fishes when it gets dark. Scared him pretty bad."

"Madison, if I hire you, you'd have to be here at 6:00 in the morning. Since you're still in school, you can leave at 7:30 and I'd want you back here when your classes end just before noon. After you graduate, I could use you full time. Summer's always busy with the tourists. I know minimum wage pay isn't much, but that's all I can afford right now. At least you'll get some experience. Are you interested?"

"Yeah. When do you want me to start?"

"How about day after tomorrow? I expect tomorrow morning will be just like it was today, everyone trying to find out what's happening and coming in here to talk and gossip. I won't have time tomorrow to explain the job to you, so let's hope it calms down day after tomorrow. Can you do that?"

"Yes, Mrs. Conner. I'll be here at 6:00 a.m. day after tomorrow. Should I wear something special?"

"No. For now you can just wear one of our aprons over your school clothes. When you start working full time, I'll get you a waitress uniform like Roxie wears. See you then."

She closed the door and turned to Roxie. "Well, at least we'll have some help. I guess she and Amber weren't the best of friends, but the way it looks, her life's already at a dead end. I feel sorry for her. Strange that her father would be the one to discover Amber."

"Yeah, poor old Dave's had to be both a mother and a father to her. I'm sure you remember when her mother left. Decided one day she didn't want to be the wife of a fisherman who was going nowhere. I heard she was a barmaid at some sleazy place outside of Portland. Don't think she gained much by leavin' the two of them," Roxie said, wiping the counter. She continued, "Well, I'm sure Dave's done the best he can do. I always felt that girl needed a mother. Maybe you can take over the job and give her some motherly advice now that your daughter's livin' in San Francisco, and I think Madison could definitely use some motherly advice."

"Uh-uh," Kelly said, straightening up the last of the tables. "I've done my time raising two children as a single mom after Mark died. Don't need to do that again. Hey, maybe you'll be the one. You've got a stepson. He could probably use a big sister. What do you think?" Kelly said, laughing, remembering all the times Roxie had told her that raising a stepson was the most difficult thing she'd ever done.

"Kelly, don't even think about it. I've got my hands full with Wade. He's been with Joe and me now for five years, ever since his mother told Joe he could have custody and raise him. I want to tell you, I could go the rest of my life and never raise another thirteen year old boy who hates his stepmother. If I didn't love Joe so much, I would have left long ago. No way would I take on anyone else. I'm gonna be doing real good to get this one raised. See you in the morning." She walked out and Kelly heard her say, "Hi, Mike. Kelly's still here. She's about ready to leave. Find out anything more?"

Kelly strained to hear his answer.

"Not much," Mike said. "Anything going on here?"

"Not that I know of, but I know Kelly talked to a lot of people. Maybe she knows something. See you later."

"Mike, I'm glad you're here. What have you found out?" Kelly said as he walked through the door.

"Not that much. Spent some time out at the Black's ranch and just like you said, Brandon's taking it pretty hard. I still can't shake the feeling that something is going on out there. Asked Jeff and Marcy all the usual questions about when they'd last seen Amber, if they'd noticed any changes in her, etc. You know, the usual stuff. Couldn't get anything from them and no one else had any information for me. Maybe the autopsy will show something. And you?"

"It was a zoo. I don't think I ever sat down from the time I got here. One thing did happen that I thought was strange, well actually two things. You know the football coach, Chris? Well, ever since he's come to town, he's come in every morning for a cup of coffee and something to eat on his way to school. He didn't come in today. I know Amber was in his English class and he probably was around her a lot because of her being head cheerleader. I imagine he was upset when he found out. Maybe that's why he was a no-show today."

"That doesn't seem too strange. I know he was close to Brandon because of football and Amber was probably a natural extension of that. I'm not particularly surprised. People deal with grief in various different ways. Some want the company of people, others prefer to be alone. Living on a boat by himself, I'd put him in the loner category, plus I've never heard of him doing anything social with anyone in town. Never even heard about him and a woman. Have you?"

"No, now that you bring it up, I've never heard of him going to anyone's house or doing anything social. Guess he is a loner and that would explain it. Here's the other thing. You know Doc, the grizzled off the grid guy? Well, he was pretty upset when he heard about Amber. It was really unlike him. And what was more unlike him was that he gave me his telephone number and asked me to call him if I heard anything. Said he'd talked to Amber several times. He left me with the impression they were friends. Sounded funny, coming from him. Don't you think that's strange?"

"Yes. Let me do a little checking on him. No one knows anything about him, although I've always liked him. I don't even know his last name. I could probably get it off of the legal records when he bought that little ranch where he lives."

"Yeah, I've always liked him, too. Got time to come by for dinner tonight?"

"Better take a rain check. It's not even twenty-four hours since Amber's body was discovered and every hour that goes by lessens the chances of finding out who killed her. Hear anything from Ginger?"

"No. I'm going to call her as soon as I get home and find out the plans for the funeral. I can't imagine planning your daughter's funeral. Thought there was some unwritten law that children were supposed to outlive their parents. Unfortunately, that family must not have gotten the message."

"Yeah. Everyone I talk to feels bad for the family. I'll give you a call later. The coroner was supposed to do the autopsy this afternoon. Maybe that will tell us something. Right now I sure can't find a motive. You're always good with people. Am I missing something? Got any ideas?"

"Not that I can think of. Only other thing would be if Amber was leading some sort of a secret life, but I sure never had a hint of that. She was every mother's dream, a beautiful young girl, straight 'A's' in school, and in love with a guy who's going to Oregon State on a football scholarship. And we can't forget she was also going to Oregon State on an academic scholarship. Sounds like a fairy tale gone bad. I remember her saying she wanted to help people and was planning on becoming a psychologist. It's such a waste!" The tears Kelly had been holding back all morning began sliding down her cheeks.

"I know, Kelly, I know. Take care of yourself. You might think about trying to take a nap this afternoon. Don't kid yourself. Telling Ginger and Brandon and then working so hard has to take its toll on you." He kissed her lightly on the cheek as he walked her to her minivan.

"Talk to you later, Babe."

CHAPTER FIVE

Kelly slept restlessly for several hours that afternoon, trying to make sense of what was happening in the small town she loved so much. She couldn't remember ever hearing about any crimes in the town other than someone stealing a pie that was cooling on a windowsill. She and Mark had felt it was the perfect place to raise their family because it was so peaceful. Now that illusion was shattered. She tossed and turned wondering why someone would kill Amber. She couldn't imagine anyone in her town doing something like that and wondered if Amber had been killed by some drifter, someone whose identity they would never know, and who'd left town immediately after committing the murder. As she lay there, she thought about Doc and Amber and wondered about their relationship. Of all the things that had happened, the fact that Doc and Amber were apparently friends seemed to be the strangest.

Her reverie was broken by the ringing of her telephone. She looked at the screen. "Hi, Mike. I took your advice and slept on and off for a few hours. Wish I could say it was the sleep of the innocent, but it wasn't. My mind is whirling. I hope you've found out something."

"Not much. Spent the afternoon talking to a lot of people who don't seem to know anything. The county coroner's report is going to take a couple more hours. Any chance I can collect on that rain check for dinner in an hour or so?"

"I'd like that. I'll call Ginger and find out what they've decided to do about a funeral service. See you soon."

She got out of bed, stood up and stretched, feeling the tension in her upper shoulders and neck. *Probably should check out that new day spa that opened a few weeks ago and have a massage. I don't just have knots in my shoulders, at the moment they feel like boulders.*

As soon as she got out of bed, Rebel stood up from his usual sentry post at the foot of her bed and walked over to the back door. He looked at her expectantly. Kelly had heard of dogs that could open doors and beer bottles. Rebel wasn't one of them. She let him out, walked into the kitchen, and took the roast, potatoes, and a biscuit can out of the refrigerator. The cheesecake could stay there until they'd finished dinner. She covered the roast and potatoes with tin foil for reheating. She figured those would be great reheated, the monkey bread not so much. She melted some butter and put grated parmesan cheese and spices into a plastic bag. She cut the biscuits into quarters, made them into balls, dipped them into the butter, and dropped them into the bag, shaking it to coat each one. She put the buttered, herb encrusted balls into an angel food cake pan and set them on the counter to rise while she turned on her upper and lower ovens. When she stood up she caught a glimpse of herself in the glass door of the microwave.

Good grief. If Mike sees me looking like this, it will probably be the last time he'll ever want to come to the house for dinner or anything else. And yeah, I'm really beginning to enjoy the anything else. She smiled to herself as she opened the door for Rebel and then walked into to the bathroom to try and minimize the effects of stress. Cold water, mascara, and lip gloss helped a lot.

A few minutes later Mike knocked and let himself in. "Kelly, I'm here and I'm hungry. What's for dinner tonight?

"Glad you're here. The Conner menu tonight features roast, potatoes, mini monkey bread, and the caramel and hot fudge topped cheesecake from last night. You must be exhausted by now. Sit down and I'll get you that glass of wine I promised you last night. Back in a minute," Kelly said.

It was early evening, the time when the color of the sky melted into the color of the ocean. When Kelly's parents built the house overlooking the bay, they took advantage of the view by having one large room on the ocean side rather than a separate kitchen, dining room, and living room. The two hundred seventy degree view of the bay and ocean was magnificent. When Kelly and Mark had moved into the house, she'd insisted on furniture that invited bodies to lounge in them rather than the uncomfortable wooden furniture that had been popular during the time her parents had lived in the house. Paintings by local artists were prominently displayed on the walls and even though it was late spring, she always had a fire blazing in the river rock fireplace. It was a simple warm, inviting home with an incredible view.

Kelly opened the wine and turned back toward Mike. Rebel had his paw on Mike's leg, inviting his ears to be scratched. As soon as Mike stopped, the paw went back on his leg. "Kelly, I swear this dog would let me scratch his ears the rest of his life, my life, or until my hand atrophied. Rebel, that's all. Off," he said. Rebel lay next to him, looking up at him with big brown eyes, hoping that the word "off" meant there would just be a momentary pause in the ear scratching.

She laughed and handed Mike his glass of wine. "I'd like to propose a toast, but don't think there's anything that great to toast right now. How about to finding out what happened?"

"Works for me. Believe me, I sure would like to. What did Ginger say about the service for Amber?"

"I talked to her sister just before you got here. Evidently Ginger's still too shaken up to talk to anyone. I understand. The service is going to be held at the church Saturday morning. Father Brown thinks a lot of people from the outskirts and surrounding towns will want to drive in for it. It's getting a lot of publicity from the local news programs as well as from as far away as Portland and San Francisco. He thought it would be better to do it on a non-week day. The family has asked some people to say a few words about her. I volunteered to have people come to the coffee shop after the service for some refreshments. Seems like people need closure at a time like this and it was the least I could do for Amber and the family."

"Awfully good of you, Kelly. I'm sure Ginger and Bob appreciate it. I did a little poking around this afternoon. Jeff Black's ranch is a lot bigger than I thought. According to the county records, he's got over two thousand acres. I thought the land he uses for his cattle operation was owned by the Bureau of Land Management, but not so. It's part of his ranch. His cattle herd sure doesn't look like it needs that many acres. Wish there was some way I could get in there."

"Mike, a thought just occurred to me. Remember I told you once that I got Rebel from the family of a narcotics drug officer who had been killed in a drug shootout? I took one look at that dog and fell in love with him. It never occurred to me to ask if Rebel ever worked with the officer as a drug dog. Maybe he'd know if there was marijuana on the ranch. I remember coming back from Phoenix once and every car had to stop at an immigration and drug check point.

"There was a helicopter, about forty officers, and even police on bridges checking out the cars before they got to the mandatory stop. The thing I'll never forget is that there was a big German shepherd dog standing between the lines of cars. It turned its head toward each car and sniffed it as the cars waited in line. Evidently he'd picked up the smell of drugs coming from one of the cars in the line because the officers were completely dismantling it and everything loaded in it. I always wondered what they'd found, if anything. Anyway, maybe Rebel could help." Rebel raised his head, acknowledging that he knew Kelly was talking about him.

"I've got some marijuana at the station. I'm holding it as evidence in a pending case. I suppose we could see if he reacts to it. I'm curious now, too. I'm going to go get it. Be back in ten minutes."

"Great. I need to put everything in the oven anyway, so take your time," she said, standing up and opening the door. "See you shortly."

Mike was back within minutes, holding a plastic bag containing marijuana. As soon as he opened the door, Rebel walked over to him and began growling. The guard hairs all along his back were raised, creating a line of jet black. He sat back on his haunches and continued to growl.

"Well, that's about all the proof I need. Only problem is, if he finds something, I wonder if it would stand up in court. You didn't train him and you don't know whether or not he was trained by some agency. Do you still have the name of the family you got him from?"

"No. After the officer's death, they left the area. That's why I got Rebel. They couldn't take him with them. I have no idea where they went. I don't even know the agency the narcotics officer was with. Sorry."

"Well, it's a start. Think I'll take him with me next time I go out to the ranch and see if anything happens."

"Mike, that's not realistic. What are you going to tell Jeff if Rebel suddenly runs out into the acreage? No, we need to come up with something else. I've got an idea."

He listened to her idea and between them, they fine-tuned it. It wasn't perfect and there was some danger involved, but it was all they could come up with.

As they were finishing dinner, Mike's phone rang. "Hi, Doc. Is the autopsy report available? It is? Great." He listened for a moment. "Yes, I can come to your office. Be there in about ten minutes. Thanks."

"Sorry, Kelly," he said, pushing his chair back from the table. "Loved the meal, but it looks like business calls. Hold the cheesecake. You know it's one of my favorites. That was the county coroner and he wants to give me the results of the report in person. That seems odd. Wonder what he's found out? Must be important if he wants to tell me about it in person. If her death was caused by drowning and a blow to the head, which we already know, I'd think he would have told me over the phone. I'll try and call you later, but it may be too late. If I can't call you tonight, I'll check with you in the morning. Forget about our plan for the Black's ranch for now. We'll try it another time. There's no hurry and I sure don't want you going out there alone."

Kelly stood at the window and watched as Mike's car pulled away. *Are you crazy*, she thought? *This is the first time since this whole thing began that I can do something that might be helpful.*

She turned and looked at Rebel. "Rebel, let's go. We're going to see if Mike's right about what's going on out at the Black's ranch."

CHAPTER SIX

As quietly as possible, headlights extinguished, Kelly drove the minivan up the long gravel driveway leading to the Black's ranch house. Even in the darkening light, she couldn't help but notice the magnificent view from the house and ranch. Sensor lights came on almost immediately, bathing the entire area in a bright blue light.

"Well, Rebel, so much for my grand plan to sneak onto the property and see if you smell any drugs. Don't think we're going to get very far with that plan. Tell you what; I'll let you out on the side closest to where the trees are. Let's see if you smell anything. I'll pretend that I stopped by to see how Brandon is doing."

She got out of her minivan and opened the passenger side for Rebel. He sniffed and just as he'd done earlier in the evening, his hackles went up and he started growling. Kelly took a deep breath and almost gagged from a revolting odor.

Good grief, how can they stand that smell? I noticed it when I was here yesterday evening, but the breeze from the ocean must have been blowing it away from the ranch. Tonight it's horrible. I read somewhere that marijuana really smells bad when it's getting close to the time to harvest it, but this is beyond what I might have expected. I wonder what the workers do. Wear gas masks? At least the Blacks can go into their house and turn on some kind of a filtering system if it's not warm enough for the air-conditioner.

Holding Rebel on his leash with one hand, she pressed the big brass door knocker three times with her other hand. The door opened so quickly she was certain that someone had been notified the moment she'd entered the driveway.

Funny, I've been out here several times during the day, but I've never noticed any type of alarm or security system. I must have activated something when I entered the driveway.

Jeff stood at the open door, looking from Kelly to Rebel. "Little late for a social visit isn't it, Kelly? And why the dog?"

"Well, I was driving by and decided to drop in and see how Brandon was doing. Rebel always travels with me. Since he hadn't been here before and he's so protective of me, I didn't want to leave him in the car, so I put him on his leash."

"Not much you can do here. Brandon's in bed, asleep, and Marcy and I were just getting ready to do the same. Thanks for coming. Understand the service for Amber will be Saturday morning. See you then," he said, closing the door.

Well, that didn't go very well, she thought. "Rebel, I'm going to pretend you got away from me. Go over to that fence and see what happens." She let the leash slide out of her hand. Rebel ran to the fence and began growling. He put his paw on the fence and was thrown back just as a gunshot rang out. She ran over to Rebel not knowing what had happened to him. The door to the house flew open and Jeff rushed over to where she was bending over Rebel.

"Kelly," he said in a menacing voice, "what's going on? What was your dog doing over by the fence?"

"I have no idea. His leash slipped out of my hand and he ran over there," she said, checking to make sure he hadn't been hit by the gunshot. "Actually, Jeff, I'd like to know what happened to my dog and why someone shot at him."

Jeff smiled in a placating manner. "Sorry, Kelly. We heard that some of the members of the Indian tribe adjacent to this property have been rustling cattle so I hired a couple of guys to make sure my cattle are safe and secure. Actually, I'd lost a few before I hired them. Don't want to point a finger, but sure is suspicious. They probably thought the rustlers sent a dog out as a scout. Looks like he's fine." He looked at the Rolex on his wrist. "It's late, Kelly. Seem to remember you have to get up pretty early. Here, let me open your car door for you. I'll watch you while you drive back to the main road. Make sure your dog doesn't try to get out, although he seems to be fine. Might want to keep a tighter grip on that leash. Hate for something to happen to him."

"Thanks, Jeff. See you Saturday at the funeral," she said as she got in her minivan and started driving back towards the road.

Jeff, you think you'd hate for something to happen to Rebel. Trust me, anything happens to this dog and you will be suspect number one. Mike was absolutely right. Something suspicious is definitely going on out here.

She called Mike and was immediately transferred to his answerphone. "Mike, it's me. You were right about the Black's ranch. I'm going home and to bed. Tell you all about it tomorrow morning and don't worry, Rebel and I are fine."

CHAPTER SEVEN

Kelly knew the residents of Cedar Bay like the back of her hand, and it was just as she'd predicted, it seemed like everyone in the small town managed to come by Kelly's Koffee Shop the next morning. She and Roxie never took a break from the time they opened until they closed. It was one customer after another, needing a cup of coffee or something more substantial. It was all they could do to make sure there was enough coffee for everyone and get things in and out of the oven in a timely manner.

While she was busy working, Kelly thought back to her conversation with Chris earlier that morning. He'd arrived at the coffee shop at his usual time and immediately walked over to her, motioning that he wanted to talk to her privately. He looked haggard, he'd missed a couple of spots when he'd shaved, and he didn't look like he'd slept.

"I couldn't come by yesterday," he said. "It was all I could do to teach class. I'm devastated by Amber's death. I can't understand why anyone would want to harm her. Do you know anything?"

"No, nothing other than what everyone else knows. I haven't talked to Mike this morning. He and the county coroner had a meeting last night, but I don't know what he found out. From what I hear it was pretty obvious that someone hit her on the head, weighted her down with some heavy free weights, and then drowned her."

"You say Mike met with the county coroner last night? Kelly, I'd appreciate if you'd do me a favor. Amber was one of my favorite students. Here's my cell phone number. Would you text me after you find out what was in the report?"

"I don't know, Chris. I'm kind of fuzzy on whether or not Mike can even give me information like that. If it's an important piece of the investigation, I doubt I'll know anything."

"Kelly, this is very important to me. Please, if you find out anything at all, let me know."

"All right, I will."

Chris left without ordering his usual two cups of coffee and ham omelet. She watched him as he walked out of the coffee house. *That's strange. He was her teacher, but she had several others. They're all upset that something like this happened to Amber, but I get the feeling there's more to it with Chris. He certainly seems to be taking it harder than the others. It's almost like he's desperate to find out what happened to Amber.*

"Sure am glad you're addicted to those bacon and chocolate chip cookies," Roxie said. "They saved us. I can't even begin to tell you how many batches I took out of the freezer and thawed out in the microwave. Seems like everyone needed a little sugar, fat, and chocolate to get through the morning. I know they've been your secret addiction for as long as I can remember, but now that your secret's out, you better keep them on hand all the time to serve the customers."

"Yeah, I was kind of thinking the same thing. Guess I'm not the only one who likes them. I remember developing the recipe after Mark died. Somehow, they soothed me in those early days of trying to cope with losing him. Pretty soon I had a stash here and another in the cookie jar at home." She laughed. "I'm embarrassed to admit it, but I even keep a private stash in the glove compartment of my minivan. Looks like they soothed a lot of the customers this morning as well."

Everyone who knew Kelly well knew she was addicted to her special recipe of bacon and chocolate chip cookies. There were always batches of them in the freezer and over the years, a few customers had learned to ask for them. They weren't on the menu, but after today she figured she'd start listing them on the large blackboard that greeted the customers as they walked in, letting them know what the daily specials were.

"See you in the morning," Roxie said, as she prepared to leave. "Joe and I have a meeting with Dr. Ramsey, the principal at Wade's school. Looks like he's been ditching his classes. Gee, there's a big surprise. I'll start to train Madison when she comes in tomorrow. You're probably going to have to bake more than usual for the big crowd that'll be here after the funeral. Bye."

CHAPTER EIGHT

Kelly decided it would be a lot easier to serve the food buffet style the next day after the funeral rather than try to serve the mourners individually. She looked around the cozy coffee shop, mentally placing where the tables should be located and what she'd put on them. The coffee, cups, napkins, plates, and silverware would work well on a smaller table. Next to it she'd have a larger table for the food and coffee.

Okay, better have plenty of comfort food on hand. Maybe that will help everyone deal with the tragedy. No matter how terrible things are, food always seems to help. I can make the sausage casserole, a French toast casserole, a couple of fruit platters, and I better have a big platter of the bacon and chocolate chip cookies. Probably ought to add a chocolate cake to that as well.

She'd almost finished her mental list when there was a knock on the door. Kelly pulled back the curtain on the small French window and saw Mike standing there. She could tell from his set jaw and the hard look in his eyes that this wasn't going to be a romance-in-the-storage-area meeting.

"Mike, come in," she said, standing on her tiptoes and lightly kissing his cheek. "I've been waiting to hear from you since early this morning. I'm so curious about what you found out from the coroner and I need to tell you about my visit to the Black's ranch and the strange conversation I had with Chris. How about some coffee or can I get you something else?"

"If you don't mind, I'll take an iced tea, pretty lady. Seem to remember you keep a pitcher of it in the frig. Actually, I'll help myself. I've been working at my computer all morning and I need the exercise."

When he returned from the kitchen, he sat down across from her. "Mike, what's wrong? What did you find out?"

Mike held the glass with one hand while he made swirling motions on the moisture on the outside of the glass with the other, then he took a deep breath, looked up at her, and began. "Kelly, did you know that Amber was pregnant?"

She half-stood then sat back down and stared at him, speechless. After a moment she said, "No. I had no idea. Does Brandon know?"

"I don't know. I can't tell him. This is a criminal investigation and I've sealed the autopsy report until the case is solved. Do you know if she was seeing someone else? I wonder if her being pregnant was the reason she was murdered and by the way, it was murder. She was hit on the head with a blunt object and a burlap bag containing three twenty pound free weights was tied to her body. Someone dumped the body in the bay, knowing she would drown, and hoped it would sink. It was a fluke that Dave happened to snag her while he was fishing and pulled her out of the water. I'm sure the murderer didn't count on that happening. The only good news is that the coroner says she was hit hard enough that she probably never came to, even when she was drowning."

In a quiet and stunned tone of voice, Kelly replied, "If she was seeing someone else, she never told me. Her best friend was Lindsay Williams, maybe she knows something. Are you going to tell Ginger and Bob?"

"No, as I told you before, this is a criminal investigation and the report is sealed. I shouldn't even be telling you, but I know you won't tell anyone and I thought you might be able to help me. You've been here longer than I have. You've grown up in this town and know everyone in it. If you come up with anything, don't hold back. Even if it's just a thought, I'd like to know."

"How far along was she?" Kelly asked.

"According to the coroner, about two months."

Kelly sat quietly looking at her hands for a moment before she spoke. "Mike, what if she was pregnant by someone other than Brandon? What if that person found out and decided to kill her. Maybe the person was married. I don't know, I'm searching here, kind of following up on when you asked me to help you, but I don't recall any married men hanging around her when she was working here."

"I don't know either, but I intend to find out. This is a small town and whoever did this can't hide forever. You mentioned you had some things to tell me. What have you found out?"

She told him about the trip she and Rebel had taken the prior night to the Black's ranch. When she finished telling him what had happened, he held up his hand. "I wasn't happy when I listened to your message. Kelly, we decided we'd do that together. Promise me you won't fly off half-cocked like that again. You're just lucky the guard didn't shoot both you and Rebel."

"Yeah, there was a moment when I realized I was in way over my head. I'm just glad it turned out okay."

He took a long drink from his iced tea. "So am I. Kelly, you mentioned Rebel jumped back from the fence. Do you think it could have been electrified?"

"Well, I hadn't thought of that, but yes, it could have been. It actually knocked him back several feet. I heard a gunshot at almost the same moment and my first thought was he'd been shot. I ran over to him and he was shaking, but there was no blood. That's when Jeff came out, and as I told you, he was not happy that I hadn't left.

41

As a matter of fact, he made a veiled threat about Rebel, something like it would be a shame if something happened to Rebel. I think that was a threat, don't you?"

"Yes. I know Rebel's always with you, but you might want to keep an eye on him when you let him outside for the next few days. You said something about having a strange conversation with Chris. Tell me about it."

"Mike, he looked terrible. He didn't come in yesterday like he always does and even though he came in today he didn't have his usual coffee and ham omelet. He said he was really shaken up over Amber. He wanted to know if you'd found out anything about her. I mentioned you had a meeting with the county coroner last night, but I hadn't heard from you. He gave me his cell phone number and asked me to text him as soon as I found out what the county coroner had told you. Don't you think that's strange?"

"Yes, but as we discussed yesterday, he probably got to know Amber pretty well between the cheerleading and her being one of his brightest students. Who knows? Maybe there's something in his past, like somebody close to him was murdered or whatever. If I've learned one thing over the years as county sheriff, it's that you never know the whole story about anyone."

"Mike, do you have a gut feeling for who did it?"

"No. I guess my prime suspect at this time is Jeff Black, but I may be prejudiced. I just don't trust the guy. I think he's up to some type of illegal activity out at his ranch and maybe committing murder wouldn't be that big of a step for him to take from what he's already doing. I was thinking on the way over here that maybe Brandon had told him Amber was pregnant and he was going to marry her. Jeff probably figured that would ruin his son's football career and the kid would be saddled with a baby and a wife when he went to college. That's not an ideal situation for a young man when he's away from home for the first time."

He continued, "I could see him doing it except for one thing. I remember someone telling me that Jeff didn't have a boat even though he lived near the ocean. Think they said as a kid he'd fallen overboard on his dad's boat and he'd never been on one since. I'm pretty sure Amber had to be dropped in the bay, probably a couple of hundred yards out from shore. There was a strong incoming tide that morning and it probably pushed her body closer to shore which allowed Dave to snag her body while he was fishing from shore that evening. Someone would have had to drop her into the ocean from a boat and I don't think Jeff could do that. I even heard he spent years going to a psychiatrist because he had such a fear of water. Believe it or not, the person told me Jeff was so afraid of water when he was younger, his parents had trouble getting him to take a shower."

"Yes, I've heard similar stories. Well, if you eliminate Jeff, what about Brandon?"

"I haven't eliminated him, but from everything I know," Mike said, "Brandon was in love with Amber. I don't see him killing her just because she'd gotten pregnant. He may not have been very happy about the situation, but I can't see him murdering her. What if Amber found out that Jeff had a marijuana farm that he covered up with his cattle operation? She was over there enough she could have discovered it. Maybe he was afraid she'd tell someone about it."

Kelly ran her index finger around the rim of her glass. "I think that's a stretch. Not many people are going to take a young woman's word over a highly respected businessman. I also seem to remember hearing that Jeff is a big political donor. Maybe people suspect what he's doing, but because of his political ties, they don't want to do anything about it. Anyway, we still don't really have a solid suspect in the case and a killer is loose in our town. That's just great, particularly with the summer tourist season about to start and don't forget, a lot of the citizens in this town make most of their money during the tourist season."

"I heard from Jimmy over at the hardware store that he had to order more door locks because people are so afraid," Mike said. "And to think this has always been a community where we all felt so safe we often left our doors unlocked."

"Yeah, I always used to leave my door unlocked," Kelly said. "The only reason I check now to see who's on the other side of the door before I unlock it and open it is because of the time the guy robbed me here at the coffee shop. Scares me even now to even think about it. He got away with one day's profits. Glad it wasn't a month's worth or I would have had to close up permanently. Believe me, the profit margin in this little old coffee shop isn't that great!"

"I know. Everywhere I go people shake their heads and can't believe something like this has happened right here in sleepy little Cedar Bay. I've got to find the murderer, if for no other reason than to make people in the town feel safe again. Kelly, I've got some resources that most people don't have. I've been working on Jeff Black all morning and when I get back to the office I should have some information on where he got the money to buy the extra acreage out at his ranch. I'm looking for offshore bank accounts and whatever else my sources can come up with. Think I'll also run a check on Chris. He's not from around here. Maybe there's something in his past that I ought to know about. Got any other ideas?"

"Yes. I told you about the strange conversation I had with Doc yesterday about Amber and him talking several times, maybe there's something in his past. Why don't you see what you can find out about him?"

"Good idea. You know, I always feel better just seeing and talking to you. Thought any more about letting me move in with you? Then I'd feel better all the time."

She laughed. "I think we've had this conversation a few times before. Love to have you visit whenever you can. It makes me happy every time I see your toothbrush in the bathroom, but if you moved in, I don't think I could ever explain it satisfactorily to Cash and Julia. They want to keep their father's memory pure and that might taint it a bit."

"Well," he said, standing up, "Let me know if you change your mind. My offer's still on the table." He pulled her to him and gently kissed her.

"Get out of here. You've got a murder to solve and if you do that much longer, I may make a decision I'd regret, and one that I know my children wouldn't like. I love you, Mike, and don't worry, you're going to solve this."

"Sweetheart, you've got more faith in me than I do," he said as he put on his Stetson and walked out to his county sheriff's car.

CHAPTER NINE

When Kelly arrived at the coffee shop early on Friday morning, Madison was already standing by the door. Roxie pulled up a minute later and the three of them entered Kelly's.

"Madison," Roxie said, "I'm going to train you today. Kelly's got enough to do getting ready for everyone coming here after the funeral tomorrow. First thing you do every morning is plug in the big coffeepot. We get it ready to go the day before. Folks will wait for anything else, but not their coffee. Here's an apron. Come with me."

The early arrivals soon began to trickle in at 7:00, thirsty for coffee and hungry for the specials. Although it was busy, the townspeople seemed to be moving on to the next most important thing in their lives. Kelly knew most of them would be back tomorrow. Even with the tragedy, no one would pass up the chance to talk to their friends and eat Kelly's food for free.

After an hour, Kelly looked at her watch and said, "Roxie, would you and Madison take over the front for me? I need to get some things ready for tomorrow or else I'll be here all night."

"No problem. Madison, fill a smaller coffeepot and whenever you see a cup that's half full, ask if they want a refill. When you finish doin' that, follow me around and I'll show you how to take an order, fill it, and run the cash register. Ready?"

Madison carried a pot of coffee into the front room. Roxie looked back at Kelly and winked. "Think we got a winner here. She's catchin' on real fast," she said as she hurried through the swinging kitchen doors and into the front room. A few minutes later Madison stuck her head into the kitchen.

"Sorry to bother you, Kelly, but Coach Chris is here and wants to talk to you. Whaddya want me to tell him?"

"Tell him I'll be there in a few minutes. I need to finish measuring the ingredients for these breakfast casseroles. If I stop now, I'll never remember where I was. Actually, when you start preparing the food, remember, if you're doing measurements, don't stop halfway through. Trust me, that's something I learned from experience. One other thing. I know I hired you to work weekdays, since that's when we're open, but is there any chance you could help me out after the funeral tomorrow? Even though we won't be serving people because it's a buffet, there's going to be so many of them here that there will be a lot of work to do like clearing plates and cups, starting the dishwasher, and replenishing the serving trays as the food gets eaten."

"Sure. When do ya' want me here?"

"I'm going to skip out of the service when the people start speaking about Amber. If you don't mind, you could come with me. I need to start the coffee and get things in the ovens. I'll cut up the fruit this afternoon and arrange it when I come in tomorrow. Sound okay?"

"I like it here. Yeah, when I see you get up during the service, I'll do the same. Oh, one other thing. I put my purse and school books in the kitchen. Is there somewhere else you'd like to me to put 'em?"

"Gosh, I'd completely forgotten that Amber had a locker here. You can use hers. I'll clean it out for you this afternoon. Just leave your things where they are for today."

A few minutes later Kelly walked out of the kitchen. Chris was standing by the cash register, looking as haggard and tired as he had yesterday. "Sorry to bother you Kelly, but I never heard from you. Did you find out what the coroner told Mike?"

"The reason I didn't text you is that Mike told me the report had been sealed as part of the criminal investigation, so I didn't have anything to tell you. Why?"

"I still can't believe it. I wish there was something I could do. It seems so wrong. I've been racking my brain trying to come with up with a motive and a name and I can't. I know all the kids in high school and I'm sure it wasn't one of them. Everyone loved Amber. It makes me sick every time I think about it. Does Mike have anyone in mind?"

"Not that I know of, but that doesn't mean much. I know there's a lot he can't tell me. Can I get you your usual?"

"I think not, but thanks anyway. I've already had way too much coffee. I was up half the night trying to get my computer to work and had no luck. It seems to be frozen. Know anyone in town who's good with computers?"

"I highly recommend Seth Morrison. His shop is down the street, about a block away. He's helped me more times than I care to remember. Don't think he opens until nine, but you might leave him a note. Good luck."

"Thanks. See you tomorrow."

True to his word, the editor of the local paper had written a eulogy about Amber and at the end, wrote about the funeral that was to take place the next day, who would be speaking, and that there would be a Celebration of Life at Kelly's Koffee Shop following the funeral. Based on the number of people who said "See you tomorrow, Kelly," as they left the coffee shop, it was going to be jammed the next day. She walked back into the kitchen and continued with the needed preparations.

Madison returned after her classes were finished and helped Roxie clean up. The three of them moved tables against the wall and set up for the Celebration of Life.

"Madison, it's two o'clock. You've really helped me a lot today. I'll see you at the service tomorrow. Oh, that reminds me, I need to get Amber's locker ready for you. Bye." Madison took off her apron and closed the door behind her.

"Kelly," Roxie said, "I know you have a lot on your mind, but is there any chance I could cry on your shoulder for a couple of minutes?"

"Of course. Let's sit down. What's up?"

"Remember I told you yesterday that Joe and I were meeting with Dr. Ramsey, Wade's principal? Well, it looks like there was more to it than an occasional ditch day. The principal didn't want to tell us over the phone, but he found almost a kilo of marijuana in Wade's school locker. Dr. Ramsey suspended Wade starting next week and he's conducting an investigation to find out if Wade was selling it to the students."

"Oh, Roxie. That's horrible. A full kilo. That's not a baggie that kids buy for personal use. With a stash that size he must have been selling it. If he's arrested, he could be sent to juvenile hall for years."

"I know. That's the first thing I thought of. Kelly, I'm so scared I don't know what to do."

"Have you told Mike? I mean, I know he's Joe's son, but if he's selling it to students, Mike needs to know. Where did he get that much?"

"Joe and I sat him down when we got home from school. It was a long night for both of us. Wade told us he got it from some guy who works out at the Black's ranch. He said everyone knows that Brandon's dad is growing it out on the back of his property."

"Well, I can't say I'm surprised that it's being grown on the ranch, but I would be surprised if Jeff knew that someone was selling it to kids at school. You know he idolizes his son and that sure could jeopardize Brandon's scholarship and future if it got out."

"I don't think Jeff knows. It sounded like one of the men who works as a guard at the ranch is selling it behind Jeff's back. I don't know. I'm so scared Wade will be arrested and kicked out of school. And then what do I do? It's bad enough when he and I are together in the evenings. I don't know what will happen if he's at home all the time."

"How's Joe taking all of this?"

"He's furious. He was so angry I thought he was going to hit Wade when he got home from school. I was able to calm him down, but I don't know how much longer I can keep peace in the family."

"Let me talk to Mike. I think it might be a good thing for you and Joe to talk to a lawyer just in case the investigation shows that Wade was selling to other students. Roxie, what do you think in your heart of hearts? I won't tell anyone."

She started to weep softly. "Kelly, I love Joe. You know that. The only reason Joe and Wade haven't come to blows is because I'm constantly acting as a bridge between both of them, trying to keep peace at home. I'm really worried that Joe will do something bad to Wade if it turns out to be true. Maybe it would be for the best. Maybe if Wade went to juvenile hall for delinquents, he'd turn around. The way he is now, I wouldn't be at all surprised if he was selling it. I wouldn't even be surprised if he was selling other drugs. I don't think Joe would like it if he knew I was talkin' to you about our troubles. He's a proud man. Proud men don't like to hear that their only son may be dealing drugs to fellow students and is on the verge of being arrested."

"Well, you probably have a few days. Amber's murder is pretty much the main topic in town right now. Let's get through tomorrow and see what happens. You know you can always call me. I'm so sorry, Roxie."

"Kelly, this is the worst thing that's ever happened to me. I thought when Wade came to live with us and turned our happy life upside down that was bad. Looking back, it was a cakewalk compared to this. Thanks for listening." As she slowly made her way to the door, Kelly thought she looked like she'd aged ten years.

I thought my life was a tragedy when Mark died and I struggled to make ends meet all those years after he died. I knew I never could afford to send my kids to college, but at least I never had to deal with what Roxie's going through. Poor dear, sweet Roxie. How my heart goes out to you.

CHAPTER TEN

By the time Kelly finished with the last of the preparations needed for the next day it was dusk. She turned off the lights and locked the door, taking a deep breath of the crisp salty air.

Darn. I forgot to clean out Amber's locker. Well, better get it over with. I don't want to lose Madison and she might think I don't care about her if I don't get her locker ready. I have a feeling I'm really going to need her tomorrow, so I want to keep her happy.

She turned around and unlocked the door, smiling to herself as she always did when she saw the Cedar Bay mementos that filled the coffee shop, adding to its charm. The locker, as she referred to it, was nothing more than a big drawer in the large storeroom located at the back of the coffee shop where she kept the dry goods, silverware, napkins, and everything that didn't need to be refrigerated or frozen.

Amber had started working for Kelly in the beginning of her senior year to earn money for college. She helped five mornings a week and in the last month had been coming in after her classes were finished just before noon to help Roxie and Kelly get ready for the next day.

Kelly opened the drawer and took out Amber's apron and a few other things that Amber had stuck in it. She got a sponge, cleaned the drawer so it would be ready for Madison, and left it open for a couple of minutes to dry out. As she turned away to rinse the sponge, she noticed something blue at the very back of the drawer. Curious, she pulled the drawer completely out and saw a small notebook wedged between the base and back of the drawer with a blue ribbon sticking out of it. She opened the notebook and read the words written in pink ink on the flyleaf page, "The Diary of Amber Cook."

Oh my gosh! This must be the diary Ginger's sister told me about. I wonder if there's a clue in here as to what happened to Amber or about her pregnancy. Too late for me to stay here any longer. I'll take it home and read it later tonight.

The only people Kelly had given her cell phone number to were Mike, Julia, and Cash, but everyone knew her home telephone number. The red light on the answerphone was blinking furiously when she got home. She spent the next hour returning calls to people who asked if they could help her tomorrow or if they could bring something. She loved the small town and its people, but as tired as she was, she would have preferred to have a glass of wine, some dinner, and go to bed. She knew the coming day was going to be emotionally and physically grueling.

Just as she finished returning the last call her cell phone rang. "Kelly, glad I caught you. I tried your home phone, but it's been busy for the last hour," Mike said.

"Everyone wants to help me tomorrow, Mike. I can't tell you how many calls I had to return. I just finished. Gonna be able to come by for dinner?"

"No. That's why I'm calling. I have a couple of appointments tonight. Things are getting interesting. I'll tell you all about it tomorrow. Anyway, you need to eat and go to bed. Tomorrow won't be easy."

"I know. I was just getting ready to do that. By the way, I found Amber's diary in her locker drawer at the coffee shop. Haven't had a chance to look at it. I'll glance through it after dinner and see what's in it."

"Kelly, I can't stop you from reading it, but you're going to have to give it to me. There may be something in it that affects the investigation. Sorry, but it's part of my job."

"I understand. Glad I thought of it. My mind's so scattered with everything I need to remember for tomorrow, I'm sure I would have forgotten about it. See you after the funeral."

"Night, Babe. Get some sleep. I love you."

I swore I would never get married again, but I'm having second thoughts, although I haven't been asked, so even thinking about it is probably just a mental exercise. I know how hurt Mike was when his wife left him. I just wish he'd believe me when I tell him I love him and we could get past it. Neither one of us is getting any younger. I need to keep reminding myself that some hurts are so deep they take a long time to heal and having your wife leave you for a guy she met on the Internet is pretty high on the hurt list.

An hour later she sat down in the large plaid chair that overlooked the bay, put her feet up on the matching ottoman and opened Amber's diary. She removed the small blue ribbon Amber used as a bookmark and that had originally caught Kelly's attention when she saw it in the drawer. She read it from start to finish then closed it and sat for several minutes, trying to make sense of what she'd just read. She wiped a tear from her eye.

Good grief. I can't believe it. Who would have ever thought? I'm stunned and feel sick to my stomach. Amber? Never in a million years would I have suspected that of Amber. I hope this diary is locked up permanently. It would kill Ginger and Bob if they read it. In some ways, I wish I'd never found it.

She let Rebel out, watching him as Mike had suggested. "Come on, boy, time for bed." He ran into the house, down the hall, and curled up in his dog bed at the foot of her bed. She turned the lights out and followed him to her bedroom.

CHAPTER ELEVEN

Kelly knew there were going to be a lot of people attending Amber's funeral, but even she was surprised by the number of cars that filled the church parking lot and overflowed onto the nearby streets. She had to park three blocks away and felt lucky to find an open spot. It was a somber occasion and no one was smiling as Amber's friends and family entered the church. She signed the guest register, took the offered memorial prayer card, and entered the sanctuary. Extra chairs had been provided and placed in every available open space. Kelly sat at the rear of the church so she could leave early and hopefully, unnoticed. Ginger and Bob, along with Ginger's sister, as well as the rest of the extended family, filled the first two rows, many of them openly weeping. She scanned the crowd for Madison who was also looking for her. She spotted Madison seated three rows in front of her, made eye contact with her, and nodded.

Good, we can both leave early and not attract attention.

She looked at the card she'd been given with the photo of Amber on it and the quote from Psalm 46:1 "God is our refuge and strength, an ever-present help in trouble." *I don't know if Father Brown or Bob and Ginger chose that, but it's certainly appropriate.*

She opened the card and read the short paragraph about Amber that was printed on the left side. The schedule for the service was printed on the right side. She'd been curious as to who would be speaking about Amber and mentally gave Brandon a lot of credit for agreeing to do it. It didn't matter how old someone was, speaking at a funeral was not easy, and when the young woman you loved had been murdered, that had to be about as bad as it gets. The principal of the high school, the student body president, and Amber's Girl Scout leader from years ago, were also listed as speakers. Looking around the church, it seemed that every student who attended the high school had come to the service. Even though there were no more seats, people continued to file into the church, standing wherever they could find space.

Kelly recognized Amber's best friend, Lindsay Williams, as she walked up to the microphone. She began the service by singing the 23rd Psalm, "The Lord's My Shepherd I'll Not Want" hymn. Kelly wiped away the tears that started sliding down her cheeks with a tissue she'd brought just for that purpose. From the sounds of sniffles and quiet crying that filled the church, she wasn't the only one with a tear in her eye.

Father Brown walked to the podium of the Catholic Church dressed in his usual white alb. A large bay window overlooking the ocean was behind him, creating a peaceful scene. He was a rather short man and could barely see over the podium. His substantial girth made it hard for him to get close enough to the podium to read his written notes. A brown fringed short beard and shaggy bangs gave him a perennial hangdog look which only made him seem all the more accessible to helping people with their real and perceived sins. He was a priest who passionately cared about his flock and they loved him for it.

One of the things that most endeared him to his parishioners was his willingness to skirt the edges of church conformity when he felt it was necessary or appropriate. Ginger and Bob had asked him if he would make the service a little more personal given the nature of the crime and the age of their daughter. He agreed with the stipulation that the traditional funeral Mass be offered. The three of them decided to have a very simple service consisting of songs, the Lord's Prayer, Mass, and a few people speaking about their remembrances of Amber.

He began, "We gather together today to support the family of Amber Cook and to pray for her and celebrate her ascension into heaven. She was taken from us at far too young an age. I don't think we need to dwell on the tragedy of her death. I hope we can all find forgiveness in our hearts for whoever took her from us. It is not us he or she will have to answer to, it is God. We can take refuge in knowing that Amber believed in God and has entered the Kingdom of Heaven, a bright shining new angel who is probably smiling down at us this very moment.

"Dealing with death is never easy for those of us who are left behind, but today we must be joyful knowing that Amber has gone home to be with her Lord. I've known Amber since she was born and I know of her deep faith. She would be the first to tell us to rejoice, that she is safe in the loving arms of the Lord. We all knew that someday she would be with the Lord, it's just that she's there a little sooner than we thought she would be."

"Ginger, Bob, we know you're in pain, but please call on us to help you get through this. We are all part of God's family and families help each other during tragedies and sad times. When you feel you can't go on, lean on our shoulders. Tell us what you need and what we can do for you. You are loved by every person in this church."

He went on to talk about his involvement with Amber from the time he had baptized her, given her First Communion, her involvement with the church youth group, and her activities in school and the community. Whenever Kelly attended a funeral service, she had the thought that these words, these accolades, should be said before people died, so they could hear the wonderful things people had to say about them. Then again maybe they could hear them.

Father Brown ended his informal remarks by asking everyone to stand, take the hand of the person next to them, and recite the Lord's Prayer. "Our Father, who art in heaven..." The words, spoken in unison, filled the church and could be heard as far out as the parking lot.

"Please be seated," Father Brown said, holding up his hands. "In accordance with the prescribed rites of the Catholic Church's funeral service, I will offer Mass this morning. When you come forward, if you are not Catholic or choose not to celebrate Mass, please cross your arms over your chest and I will give you a blessing. Following the completion of Mass, several people have been asked to speak about Amber. To conclude the service, we will sing Amazing Grace. You are all welcome to attend the Celebration of Life for Amber which is being held at Kelly's Koffee Shop immediately after the service is completed. There are flyers with directions at the rear of the church." After the Mass was completed Father Brown announced that the first speaker would be Brandon Black.

Kelly would have liked to hear what Brandon had to say, but knew she couldn't stay any longer. She stood up and walked out the door. In a moment she heard Madison's voice beside her. "Hi, Kelly. Wasn't that beautiful? I don't go to church, but after today, I think I will."

As Kelly opened the door of her minivan for Madison, she patted Rebel on the head. He always stood looking out the car window in the direction he'd last seen her go until she returned. "Father Brown is a wonderful man. I've been attending his services for a long time and I always feel better afterwards. Are you ready for a busy day?"

"Yeah. People found out that I'm workin' at the coffee shop and it seems everywhere I went yesterday afternoon, people asked if I was going to be workin' for you today. I know you can estimate how much food to prepare so you don't waste any, but I just hope there's enough to go around."

"I'll let you in on a secret. I didn't sleep much last night worrying about the same thing, but I'm pretty sure we'll be all right. I stayed at the coffee shop several hours after you and Roxie left yesterday, making extra casseroles, just in case. If we don't use them today, we can always freeze them for next week. Believe me, with everything that needed to be refrigerated, I'm really glad I invested in a walk-in refrigerator. There's no way all of that food could fit into a regular one! Here we are and I see Roxie pulling in behind us. I'd like you to plug in the big coffee pot and start the ovens at 350 degrees. Also turn on the warming ovens. Oh, by the way, I cleaned out Amber's locker for you so you can put your purse in it. It's the large drawer to the left as you walk into the storeroom."

I've got to remember to tell Mike about the diary after the Celebration is over. I put it in my purse when I left the house. When he hears what's in it, it's definitely going to be part of his investigation.

Kelly and Roxie arranged the fruit platters and put them in the walk-in refrigerator. They took large serving dishes out of the cabinets and arranged the casserole slices on them.

"Roxie, do me a favor. Would you take a couple of batches of the bacon chocolate chip cookies out of the freezer and arrange them on platters? It won't take long for them to defrost. I can't be trusted. I'd probably eat them all if I tried to do it."

"Sure. I like them, but I can at least resist them, unlike some people I know," she said, grinning at Kelly. "My green thumb has begun to sprout all kinds of flowers in my yard. I brought several bouquets with me. They're in the car. Thought they might brighten the tables. Okay with you if I arrange them?"

"Oh, Roxie, I never even thought about flowers. Thank you so much! Flowers always cheer people up. You know where the vases are in the storage room."

A few minutes later the door opened and the first guests arrived. For the next three hours, Kelly's was a kaleidoscope of people, food, conversations, tears, and laughter. It seemed like everyone who had known Amber, had heard of Amber, or had read about the murder, had come to the funeral, and then on to Kelly's.

Although Mike's name had not been listed on the card as a speaker at the funeral, when the last speaker had finished, Father Brown asked if anyone else wanted to say a few words. Several people told her that Mike went to the podium and spoke to everyone about how wonderful Amber was and reassuring them that a massive investigation for the killer was under way. He said he was not at liberty to share any facts about the investigation because of its criminal nature, but his office had been given information that he was certain would lead to the arrest and conviction of the killer. It was a heartfelt speech, and even though no one in the church wanted to hear the word "killer," everyone was glad that Mike was confident the guilty person would soon be brought to justice.

After the last guest had left the coffee shop, Mike sat in the corner, looking at his email on his phone while Kelly profusely thanked Roxie and Madison for their help. "Ladies, I can't thank you enough. I know you both must be exhausted. I know I am. Get out of here and I'll see you Monday. I don't know if it's proper to call a Celebration of Life successful, but if the amount of food eaten is any indication, it was a huge success. I thought I'd prepared enough food to last us through next week, but I was wrong. From the limited number of leftovers you two put away, I think I'll have to spend tomorrow afternoon cooking for next week. Again, many thanks!"

CHAPTER TWELVE

Kelly closed the door behind Roxie and Madison, locked it, and then turned to Mike. "I hear you gave a wonderful speech at the service. Several people told me they felt much safer after listening to you. I'm sure it wasn't easy for you, but it probably had to be done."

"Well, when I heard how many door locks Jimmy had sold and how afraid people were, I didn't really have a choice. The memorial prayer cards were printed yesterday afternoon and by the time I contacted Father Brown and told him I'd like to say a few words, it was too late. Gracious as always, he gave me an entry. The man not only looks like a saint, he is! Now, tell me about the diary."

"Let me get it. I think you're definitely going to want to keep it." She went into the storeroom to get her purse and returned a moment later. "Here it is. Before you open it, I have to tell you that I read it."

"You know I would have preferred it if you hadn't, but as curious as you are, I never that doubted you'd read it. And…"

"Mike, she knew she was pregnant. According to the diary, she'd been having an affair with a man, but she never said who it was. She wasn't sure whether Brandon or this mysterious lover was the father. She was torn as to whether she should tell Brandon the baby was his, knowing he would marry her right away. Amber felt it was her fault she'd gotten pregnant because she'd lost her birth control pills. She didn't want to tell Ginger she'd been taking them and the doctor she'd originally gotten them from had left the area. She didn't know what to do. She was afraid Oregon State would revoke Brandon's scholarship if he was married and had a baby and she also made a reference to some serious tension between Brandon and his father. She was afraid his dad would be furious. She also said if his dad got really mad at Brandon, then Brandon might tell the authorities and it would ruin the family, whatever that means."

"Whoa, Amber said that there was tension between Brandon and his father? That might explain why Jeff wanted to know if Amber had ever said anything about the ranch. What else?"

"She referred to Doc. Said she'd talked to him a couple of times about 'it.' Don't know what she meant by that."

"I think I might. When you're finished I'll tell you."

"Well, the other thing that was interesting is that she mentioned she gave her mysterious lover half of her blue cheerleading ribbon. She said in her diary that he'd wanted a memento of her. You know, the cheerleaders all get them at the beginning of the season and the head cheerleader gets a special one. It's a real status symbol of 'being somebody' in high school. I remember years ago when Julia would talk about a cheerleader wearing the blue ribbon. It was a really big deal. The other thing that's scary is she mentioned she decided to tell her mysterious lover about her pregnancy, figuring he'd know about it in another month or so anyway. Evidently she was also torn about having an abortion, probably because of being raised in the Catholic Church. That's about it."

Mike sat quietly for several moments, absorbing what she'd said. "Kelly, I ran a check on Doc. I found out his last name is Burkhart. He came here from a small town in Southern California. Evidently he performed an illegal abortion on a young girl and she died. Her parents didn't know she was pregnant and he wanted to help her. The circumstances are pretty similar to those involving Amber. It was the girl's senior year in high school and she'd been accepted at a top college. He was charged in criminal court with manslaughter, but he was acquitted, however, the State Medical Board felt there was enough evidence to revoke his license. His wife left him and he moved here. No wonder he wants to be off the grid."

"Mike, you don't seriously think Doc had something to do with Amber's murder do you? Why, he seems like one of the gentlest men I've ever met."

"At this point I can't rule out anyone. Oh, one other thing. The hero of the high school, Coach Chris," he said sarcastically, "was arrested in Utah on child pornography charges. He was fired from his job at the high school and came to Cedar Bay for a new start. The mother of a young girl who was a student of his happened to be looking in her daughter's purse for some lipstick she thought her daughter had borrowed from her. She found photographs of her nude daughter and the coach which had been taken off the Internet from one of those porn sites. Talk is he paid off the mother, who was very poor. After that the mother and the girl refused to testify against him and the charges were dropped. He must have used some phony references to get the job here in Cedar Bay, although I have to say he's done a darn good job for the school."

"I can't see how that ties in to Amber. Sure, he was her teacher, but we don't know of anything else. Oh Mike, I just thought of something. He was in here yesterday, as frazzled looking as he'd been the day before. He made light of it and claimed he'd been up most of the night trying to fix his computer which seemed to be frozen. He asked if I knew any repairman. I gave him Seth Morrison's name. You don't think he and Amber...?"

"I don't know what to think, but several pieces of the puzzle are beginning to fall into place. I also found out something else that disturbs me. Evidently Madison told a few people she wished Amber was dead because she'd stolen Brandon from her, was homecoming queen, and head cheerleader. When I heard that, I became a little concerned for your safety."

"Mike, Madison has been a huge help. She couldn't have done it."

"Who knows? Just because she's young doesn't mean much. Some of the worst murders in history have been committed by young people. Plus, maybe she somehow found out that Amber was pregnant and she was sure Brandon would marry her. Jealousy is always a powerful motive."

"If my head is reeling, yours must be doing flip-flops, going from one suspect to another. Why don't you take the rest of the day off?"

"Yeah, I feel like I have all these voices inside my head screaming at me. I'm tired and when I'm tired, there's a good chance I'll overlook something. I'm not going to do anything about the case this afternoon. People need a little time to recover from the funeral and spend time with their families."

"Well, my good sheriff, how about spending the rest of this beautiful day relaxing on my deck, doing nothing more important than looking at the bay? I'll make us a nice dinner and you might even think about making use of that toothbrush I keep on hand for occasions like this."

"Lady, I like the way you think. Meet you at your house."

He took his Stetson from the coat rack and they walked out the door hand in hand, looking forward to what the night would bring.

*****

"Mike, I hope you feel as good as I do this morning," Kelly said as she got out of bed Sunday morning. "Stay here and rest. I'll treat you to breakfast in bed in a few minutes. I know you're probably anxious to get home or to the office and sift through everything, but if you can, hang around and I'll wrangle up a great breakfast for you. Besides, I like having you here and it gives me an opportunity to be close to you."

"Breakfast in bed? Lady, you know how to start a man's day out right. Trust me, I'm not moving."

Kelly brushed her teeth, threw on a pair of jeans and a T-shirt, and was in the kitchen in minutes. *Okay, after last night he's got to be hungry,* she thought. *I know I am.* She smiled, remembering their lovemaking. *Okay, back to this morning. Let's see. Sourdough buttered toast, a mushroom omelet, and a thick slice from the ham we had for dinner last night. That should do it. Oh, and I brought home some of that leftover fresh fruit from the coffee shop. Perfect.*

"Sit up, lazybones. Your private chef and waitress is providing you with morning sustenance. Enjoy," she said, handing him the tray of food. "I'll be back in a minute with today's paper and coffee."

Kelly loved to begin Sunday mornings by reading the San Francisco Chronicle. She subscribed to the local paper, but the problem with it was she already knew about almost everything that was printed in it. She usually read it in five minutes, but the Chronicle was her weekly indulgence. She stayed up to date on books, movies, and the news of the day, both domestic and international. When she finished reading the paper, she spent an hour doing the crossword puzzle, or attempting to do it. Long ago she made a promise to herself that if she ever finished a Sunday crossword, she'd sell the coffee shop and travel to Italy. She knew there wasn't much danger of that happening and that's why she only subscribed on Sundays. She could justify not finishing the Sunday puzzle, but if she wasn't able to finish the ones during the week, it might seriously depress her. She'd rather not know.

"Kelly, I've got a lot to do today, but last night and this morning were just what I needed. Keep this up and I might have to make an honest woman out of you."

"A few more nights like last night and I won't care whether or not you make an honest woman out of me," she said smiling and ruffling his hair. "I've got to spend the afternoon at the coffee shop and get ready for the week. After yesterday, I don't know how much I have of anything. I can certainly use the exposure the Celebration gave the coffee shop, but my regular customers expect their favorites and I need to keep them happy."

"Rebel, you take care of this wonderful lady. Kelly, I'll talk to you later," Mike said as he left the house and headed for his car. Rebel whined as he and Kelly stood at the door, watching Mike back out of the driveway.

Well, it will probably be all over town that I didn't go to church this morning and that Mike obviously spent the night. Oh, what the heck. We're two consenting adults and I know the only thing Father Brown will do the next time he sees me is smile.

CHAPTER THIRTEEN

As soon as Kelly and Rebel walked into the coffee shop, she picked up Rebel's bed and carried it to the kitchen. "You can stay here this afternoon. I've got a lot of baking to do." She checked her supplies, called Lucy at the Cedar Bay Market and gave her a list of what she needed. "I'll come by later and pick the order up. I need to spend some time cooking here at the coffee shop and then I need to run an errand," she told Lucy.

Several hours had gone by when she turned to Rebel and said, "Rebel, I can't get this out of my mind. I know Mike wouldn't approve, but you and I are going to pay a little visit to Doc. I just can't believe he has any involvement in this, but I need to find out."

Although she'd never been to Doc's she had a good idea where he lived. He'd made occasional references to his ranch when they'd talked at the coffee shop and she remembered him saying he'd painted the front door of his house red because it was supposed to bring good luck. She also remembered him saying he liked the name of the lane the ranch was on, Serenity Summit Lane. She took out her iPhone and silently blessed Google Maps as it showed her exactly where Serenity Summit Lane was located.

"Let's go, Rebel. I mean, how difficult can it be to find a house that has a red door and is on Serenity Summit Lane?"

Ten minutes later she turned onto the lane from the main road. Doc's ranch was at the end of the lane along with several other small ranches. His old pickup was in the driveway. She pulled into it and turned off the engine.

She was just opening the minivan door when Doc walked around from the side of the house. She waved to him and got out.

"Kelly, to what do I owe the pleasure of a visit from you and Rebel?" he asked, opening the door so Rebel could get out. Rebel liked Doc and immediately rubbed his head against Doc's leg, indicating he wanted his ears scratched, while at the same time earnestly wagging his tail. "Come in. I just made some lemonade from the lemons on the tree I have on the back patio. Rebel, you too." He opened the front door for them.

"Doc," she said, looking around the living room. "You never mentioned you were an antique collector, although I certainly can see why you wouldn't want people to know what you have out here. I don't know much about antiques, but this furniture looks a lot like some Arts and Crafts pieces I recently saw on television. And these paintings! They're incredible. I remember the host on that show talking about California Impressionist paintings. Is that what these are?"

"Yes. All of this comes from my grandparents. I don't talk much about my personal life, but I'm divorced. My wife wanted these pieces and some others I'll show you, but I had a very good attorney who made the case that this was my separate property since I'd inherited it. They make me happy and remind me of my family."

"Oh, Doc, here, this is for you. I had an extra crumble coffee cake and I know how much you like it. Thought I'd bring you some. It was just taking up space in the walk-in. Enjoy," she said handing him the cake.

"How thoughtful of you! Come on, I'll give you the grand tour."

She followed him, amazed at the quality of the antiques and

artwork he had in the old ranch house. A Tiffany lamp and brightly colored pottery were only a few of the beautiful decorative pieces.

"Doc, I had no idea. I feel like I'm in a museum. I think I should put Rebel in the car. As big as he is, if he bumped into anything and broke it, I'd never forgive myself. It's a good thing I don't have any young children with me! Rebel, lie down," she said in an assertive voice. She turned back to Doc. "It will make me feel better if he's at least lying down."

"Let's go into the kitchen and sit down. Rebel, come," Doc said, taking the lemonade out of the refrigerator. He turned towards Kelly. "I really appreciate the coffee cake, but I have a feeling you have some other reason for being here."

Kelly was quiet for a few moments, taking several sips of her lemonade. "Doc, this is delicious. You're right. I do have an ulterior motive for being here. A couple of weeks ago a tourist was in the coffee shop and after you left, asked to speak to me," she said, silently apologizing to the gods of truth for what she was about to say. She knew she couldn't tell him Mike had been the source of what she knew about him.

"He asked your name and said you looked familiar. I told him your name was Doc. He said, 'That's it. I knew I'd seen him before, but I just couldn't place him. I live in Southern California and his name and picture were in the newspapers and on television for several weeks a couple of years ago. He was accused of performing an illegal abortion on a young woman and she died. Even though he was arrested and stood trial, he was acquitted. The State Medical Board took away his license to practice medicine. I always wondered what happened to him.' I told him I didn't know anything about it and that was all he said. With everything that's happened recently, I forgot about it. This morning I woke up, worried that someone might have overheard him and that you could become a person of interest in the investigation of Amber's death. I guess I'm here to warn you, but I'd also like to know what you and Amber talked about."

Doc stood up, walked over to the window and stood there for several minutes. Finally he turned to Kelly and said in a low, faltering voice, "Kelly, thank you for coming and having the courage to tell me about your conversation with the customer. Let me tell you what happened. This won't be easy because it was a very painful time for me. I saw no reason to tell anyone here in Cedar Bay about my past. As a matter of fact, other than having lunch at your coffee shop, I haven't had much interaction with anyone in the community. A little over three years ago a patient of mine, I was a general practitioner for a large HMO in Southern California, came to my office and told me she thought she was pregnant. She was a young girl who had just turned seventeen. Her parents were very strict and had no idea that she and her boyfriend were having sex.

"The HMO I worked for was very opposed to underage women obtaining birth control pills, even though legally in California a minor could obtain them without the parent's consent. I wasn't allowed to prescribe them. I examined her and confirmed that she was pregnant.

"To say she was panicked would be the understatement of the year. She was a senior in high school and had been accepted to a prestigious Eastern college. Her boyfriend was the star quarterback on the football team and they seemed to be very much in love. After my first consultation with her, I had several more appointments with her. She begged me to abort the baby. I told her that when I was hired by the HMO, I had signed a sworn statement that I would never perform an abortion while I was working there. She told me if I didn't help her, she didn't know what she was going to do. She said a friend of hers was willing to take her to Mexico and have it done there, even though she easily could have gotten one through a number of agencies in California. She was afraid if she had it done anywhere in California, her parents would find out about it. Her father was a very well-known politician and she knew his opponents would pounce on this kind of information and use it against him."

"Doc, I don't know what I would have done in that situation. I can't imagine how you must have felt."

"I struggled with that decision more than anything I've ever struggled with in my life and ultimately, I made the wrong decision. I knew she was going to have it done no matter what and there was a good chance a botched abortion would mean she would never be able to have children or even worse, she might die. I told her I would do it. I had a friend who was a doctor in private practice. I called him and asked if I could use his office. I performed the abortion and it went very well. There were no complications whatsoever. She had a friend take her home and I thought that was the end of it. I was wrong."

"Why do I feel like the other shoe's about to drop?" Kelly asked.

"Because it did. That night the young woman started hemorrhaging and before her parents could get medical help, she died. Her parents found my business card in her purse with the address where she was to go for the abortion. The police went to the address, realized it was a medical facility, and called my friend, the doctor who owned it. He told them I had called him and asked if I could see a patient in his office. He didn't know why I was seeing the patient or what I intended to do while using his office. I really don't blame him for telling them. It was him or me. I was arrested and charged with manslaughter. To make a long story short, a trial was held, but I had a magnificent attorney who was able to convince the jury that although she died and the autopsy showed she'd had an abortion, there was no link between any alleged malpractice on my part and her death. In layman's terms, her death was caused by a freak of nature, a blood vessel which broke after she returned home and had nothing to do with the abortion."

"Doc, I'm surprised that the family would agree to your being charged with manslaughter, given the father's high political profile. I can't imagine they would want publicity like that."

"They didn't want the publicity, but it was out of their hands. They weren't the plaintiffs, the State of California was. It was a criminal trial, not a civil trial. When they realized they couldn't do anything about it, they turned it to their advantage and made a media circus event out of it - grieving mother and father, sweetheart of a young girl, evil doctor who performed an abortion. You get the picture. The politician played it beautifully. It was an election year and he won by a landslide. When it was over, my wife left me and took our two teenage sons, who wanted nothing to do with me. I packed up and left town. I drove all over the west coast, looking for a place to land. Fortunately, I'd inherited some money from my parents, so I didn't have to work. I found Cedar Bay and here I am."

"I'm curious what you and Amber talked about."

"Kelly, Amber was pregnant. She and I talked occasionally at the coffee shop when she came in after school to help you. One day she was waiting for me in the parking lot when I pulled in at the usual time. She wondered if I was named Doc because I was a real doctor. I told her I was, but that I was no longer practicing medicine. I told her I'd retired. I thought that was the end of it. It wasn't. The next day she was waiting for me at the same time. She asked if she could come out to the ranch and talk to me about something. I liked her and I knew that it must be important if she wanted to talk to me privately at the ranch."

"I can't believe Roxie and I missed seeing the two of you in the parking lot two days in a row. Guess I'm not as good at noticing what's up with people as I thought I was."

"Don't feel bad. Both times were very short. Anyway, that afternoon she came out to the ranch. To make a long story short, she told me she was pregnant and she was debating whether or not to have an abortion. She told me she was struggling with it because of her deep religious faith. She went on to say it would kill her parents if she kept the baby because it would mean she couldn't go to college and they'd been so proud of her, but as strong Catholics, it would kill them just as much if she had the abortion. I told her what had happened to me in California when I'd performed an abortion on a young woman. We really bonded that afternoon. I felt in some ways like she was the daughter I'd never had."

"I'll be back in a minute Doc. I need a Kleenex. This is so, so sad." She returned, blowing her nose with her eyes much brighter than usual. "Please go on."

"It was like 'déjà vu'. I told her if she made the decision to have an abortion, I would be happy to give her information, but that I would not do an abortion on her under any circumstances. When I heard she'd died, that was my first thought, that she'd gone ahead and had an abortion and someone had botched it. Then I heard she'd been murdered. I don't understand why anyone would want to kill her."

"Doc, did she tell you who the father was?"

He looked at her, shocked she would even ask the question. "No. It never occurred to me to ask. I assumed it was that football guy she goes with. I think his name is Brandon Black. Do you think someone else could have been the father?"

"I don't know. I'm trying to look for a motive, but I'm sure not finding one. I have a hard time believing that Brandon murdered her. There must be someone else. Doc, I hate to say this, but if people find out about your past and her pregnancy, even though it looks like she didn't have an abortion, you really might become a person of interest in the murder investigation."

"Yes, that was my first thought when I heard about it. That's why I asked you to tell me anything you knew. Besides me, you're the only one who knows she was pregnant and had asked me for advice. She told me she hadn't even told Brandon because she wanted to make the decision on her own. You're also the only one who knows that I told her about my past. Kelly, I know you and Mike are close, but since I had nothing to do with Amber's murder, I would ask that you not tell him about this conversation."

"I won't, Doc," she said, inwardly crossing her fingers. *Sheesh, two major lies in one day. The next time I walk into church every bell will probably ring, letting everyone know I'm a liar.* "Doc, it's getting late and I need to pick up an order from Lucy, drop it off at the coffee shop, and get some sleep. Thanks for talking to me and I'm so sorry about what happened to you. I wish I could think of some way you could use all that good medical knowledge you have. Seems like a shame to waste it."

"I've thought the same. If you come up with an idea, let me know. Rebel, time for you to go. Kelly, mind if I give him a little treat?"

"No. It's past his dinner time anyway." At the words "dinner time," Rebel's tail began wagging and he walked over to Doc who had opened the refrigerator.

"Rebel, sit," Doc said. He cut a piece of meat for Rebel and handed it to him. Even though Rebel weighed ninety pounds, he delicately took it from Doc's fingers.

"Doc, that looks like a filet mignon steak. Did you just give my dog filet mignon?"

"Yeah," Doc said sheepishly. "It's one of my vices."

"Well when I feed him and he won't eat his canned dog food, I'll be thinking evil thoughts of you," she said laughing. "Come on Rebel, time to go. Doc, I'll see you tomorrow and thanks for the tour. With these beautiful things, you might think about getting a couple of guard dogs yourself."

"Been tossing the idea around, Kelly. I'll let you know if I do. Course if you ever want to get rid of Rebel, you know where to come. See you tomorrow."

CHAPTER FOURTEEN

The next morning Rebel's growl woke Kelly up a few minutes before her alarm clock was scheduled to go off. He was standing by the open window, guard hairs raised all along his back, creating a dark line. "What's up, Rebel? Something wrong?" He continued the low, rumbling sound. She stood up and walked over to the window.

"Okay, I smell it too. Must be a fire somewhere. I'll get dressed and we'll go outside."

There was a faint orange glow coming from what appeared to be a fire off in the distance. She heard the sound of sirens and wondered where the fire was located.

Strange time of year for a fire. They usually happen in late fall, long after the rains have stopped and everything becomes dry. Well, I'm sure I'll hear all about it at the coffee shop this morning. This will be big news. Fires and forests don't mix and there's plenty of forest land around here.

*****

"Morning, Madison, Roxie," she said, unlocking the coffee shop door. "Hope you both got a chance to relax yesterday. Either one of you know what's going on? I heard sirens when I got up and I can still hear them. That glow in the sky sure looks like it's coming from a pretty good-sized fire outside of town somewhere."

"No," they answered in unison, with looks of concern on their faces.

"It's got to be a pretty big fire," Roxie said. "Just as I was leaving the house the phone rang and I overheard Joe say he'd be right there. He's a volunteer fireman. When the county fire department starts calling for reinforcements from other areas, they also alert the volunteers. I'll call Joe later on and see what's going on."

On mornings like this, the citizens of Cedar Bay found comfort in talking to one another. They were actively discussing the finer points of the funeral service. Several of the conservative Catholics were not happy that Father Brown had chosen to conduct the service in a more relaxed manner. They preferred things to be the way they'd always been. Others felt it was a beautiful service and perfect for a young woman that was as well-liked as Amber. The debate went on and on.

Chris showed up as usual, sat at the counter and ordered a ham omelet from Roxie while she poured his coffee. When Kelly walked by, he said, "I want to thank you for referring me to Seth Morrison. He's pretty sure he can fix my computer, but he'll have to keep it a couple of days. Didn't realize how dependent I'd become on that darn thing to give me news and entertainment. I don't even own a television set. I just use my computer."

"I know what you mean. I can't believe how things have changed in the last few years. I'm always amazed by how many kids I see crossing streets or walking while they're looking at their phones."

"Kelly, I'm a teacher. Can you imagine what would happen in a classroom if nobody turned off their phones during class? I mean, think about it. Every one of them has a phone they've put some new song on as the ring tone. Or even a different song for different people who call them. The first thing I have to do every morning is remind them to turn off their phones. I was glad to know when I came here about the strict policy the county school superintendent has on phones. If someone's phone rings during class, that person is immediately sent to the principal's office. If it happens a second time, he or she is suspended from class for the rest of that school week. If it happens a third time, they're expelled. It's harsh, but it sure works."

"Well, it's time for me to get back to work, but it's been good seeing you, Chris. Glad you're back. I need to pull some things from the ovens. See you tomorrow."

As the morning wore on, the talk turned to what seemed to be a very large fire. No one knew where it was located. From time to time sirens could still be heard in the distance. Wherever Kelly went, Rebel was right behind her. He sensed fires were dangerous and since his self-appointed job in life was to insure her safety, he stayed right next to her. Over the years, the customers had grown used to watching out for him. Tripping over a ninety pound dog with not an ounce of fat on him was like tripping over a brick wall. Kelly realized there was no way the dog was going to get in his bed until the fire was out and there was no threat of danger. She picked up his bed and took it to the storage room.

Late that morning, Roxie's husband, Joe, opened the door of the coffee shop. He was sweaty and covered with soot. "Kelly, where's Roxie? I need to talk to her."

"She's in the kitchen."

A few minutes later they both hurried out of the kitchen, Roxie untying her apron. "Kelly, is it okay if I leave early? Something's come up at home. I'll call you later."

"Of course, sweetie. Anything I can do?"

"No, but the fire was at the Black's ranch. Looks like it pretty much burned it up."

"What?" she exclaimed, but by that time Roxie and Joe had left.

A fire at the Black's ranch? Now what? Mike will know what's happening. She walked into the kitchen, took her phone from her purse and called him.

"This is Mike," the voice said. "I can't take your call right now. Please leave your name and number and I'll get back to you." She asked him to call and walked back into the main room.

It was the tail end of the lunchtime crowd and not many people were left in the coffee shop. A few of them had heard Roxie say something about the fire being at the Black's ranch and asked Kelly if Roxie had told her anything more.

"No, and I tried to call Mike, but all I got was his answerphone. I don't know any more than you do. If he calls, I'll let you know."

The last of the diners left, several of them saying they were going to drive out to the Black's ranch and see what happened. Others were anxious to get on their phones and see what they could find out. In most small towns gossip was the main entertainment and Cedar Bay was no exception. It was fast, efficient, and sometimes right. It reminded Kelly of the old Tarzan movies and the drumbeat messages sent by the local natives.

Madison helped Kelly for the next two hours, cleaning up and getting ready for the next day. Kelly knew the fire danger was gone when Rebel consented to get on his bed while she made the breakfast casseroles. There was only a faint smell of smoke in the air. She couldn't wait to talk to Mike.

CHAPTER FIFTEEN

When Kelly got home, the first thing she noticed was the blinking red light on her answerphone. "Kelly, it's Roxie. Sorry I bailed on you today. Give me a call when you have a chance. I need to talk to you."

The events of the last week had taken their toll on Kelly's house and on her newly planted spring garden flowers. Both called out for attention and Kelly had mentally promised herself that today was the day she'd take care of them. After hearing Roxie's message, she wasn't so sure she'd be able to keep her promise.

Kelly changed her clothes and called Roxie. "Hi Roxie, I got your message. Is everything okay?"

"Yes and no. I told you the fire was out at the Black's ranch. From what Joe told me, looks like some dry brush caught fire and the fire was probably intentionally set by someone. The cattle herd Jeff has on the ranch is just for show. His real business is the marijuana he was growing. The fire spread to the back part of the ranch where he was growing it. The marijuana caught fire and everything burned to the ground."

"Oh, my gosh!"

Roxie continued, "The only things that were spared were the cattle and the ranch house. Joe says it's like scorched earth back there. Nothing left but ashes. Not a single plant was left standing. They were just incinerated by the extreme heat of the fire. The barn and everything else completely burned to the ground. Mike arrested Jeff Blake for having an illegal marijuana farm on his property and put him in the county jail. I understand he's trying to make bail. Mike told me he'll be arraigned tomorrow and then a trial date will be set or he can do some type of plea bargain, but for now he's in jail."

"You said Mike told you that. When did you see him? You didn't go out to the Black's ranch did you?"

"No," Roxie said. "Here's the next part of the story. Brandon heard that Wade had been suspended from school for having marijuana in his locker. You know how fast news spreads in this town, particularly among school kids. Anyway, he also heard that Wade had purchased the marijuana from one of the guards out at Black's ranch. He told Jeff about it and Jeff was furious. He called the guard into his office and fired him. Evidently he was worried that someone could trace Wade's marijuana to his ranch. The next part is pretty hard for me to understand. Brandon told Mike that he'd known for a long time that his dad was growing marijuana on the ranch, but Jeff justified his actions by telling him he only sold it to medical marijuana shops and that it was perfectly legal."

"Mike's suspected that Jeff was growing it for a long time, but couldn't prove it. Looks like he was right," Kelly interrupted.

"Yeah, but here's what I started to tell you. Even though he grew it and probably made a lot of money from it, he was completely opposed to anyone using it for recreational purposes. That's why he fired the guard."

"That makes no sense at all. You're telling me he didn't want kids to use it, but it was okay for him to make a profit from it?"

"Yep, that's what I understand. The guard Jeff fired died in the fire. Mike thinks he started the fire to get back at Jeff and then the fire got out of control. Evidently he got trapped and couldn't get out. The county fire department has called in some experts to see where the point of origination was and to confirm if it was arson."

"Okay, but I still don't see why and how Mike told you all of this."

"I'm getting to it. Give me a minute. When Joe came to the coffee shop, he told me Mike wanted to meet with us about Wade and the kilo of marijuana they'd found in his locker. Sorry, Kelly, but that was more important to me than staying at the coffee shop."

"No apologies needed. I would have done the same. Well, what happened?"

"Mike met us at our house and asked us to get Wade. He said he wanted to talk to all of us. Today was the first day of Wade's suspension, so he was in his room. The four of us sat down in the living room and Mike told us what he had learned. He said the principal contacted him late yesterday about Wade having marijuana in his locker. Mike also said it was kind of ironic, because he was planning on going out to the Black ranch this morning to talk to the guard and Jeff about it. He asked Wade if he was using drugs. Wade said no, but he had sold some of the marijuana to other kids at the school."

"Well, I know it happens, but I'm sorry Wade got involved."

"So am I, then Mike asked Wade a few more questions. He wanted to know what made him start selling pot to the students. Wade said that for the first time he was getting some attention from the other kids. He told Mike that no one cared about him, not his mother, his father, or me. He said it was nice to finally have someone pay attention to him. Kelly, I couldn't help myself. I started crying and telling him how much Joe and I loved him and that I didn't know why he felt that way. I guess in his eyes I haven't been a very good stepmother. I think all the kid wanted was to feel accepted by us and since he didn't feel that we accepted him, in some crazy way I guess he thought if he sold pot to the kids, they'd accept him.

"Anyway Mike said if Wade promised him he would never sell it again and if the three of us got family counseling, he had the authority, as county sheriff, not to file charges against Wade. He said he would get in touch with the principal and Wade could go back to school tomorrow. He told all three of us that if we didn't go to counseling, or if he even heard that Wade was dealing or doing drugs, he would not only make sure he was prosecuted, but he would talk to the authorities and strongly suggest that he be sent to juvenile hall."

"Oh, Roxie, that's wonderful. I'm so happy Wade's not going to be prosecuted, but what are you and Joe going to do about Wade to make him feel better about being part of the family?"

"The three of us had a long talk after Mike left. I was honest and I think Joe and Wade were as well. Bottom line is Wade didn't think we wanted him to live with us. His mother had told him that Joe had left her for me, so he resented me for stealing his father and breaking up his parent's marriage. Joe and I never knew that. Now that we do, I think we understand why he's acted like he has and he probably thought the kids would think he was a big deal because he sold pot."

"Wow! Well, the whole thing was probably a blessing in disguise. Now you know how he's felt all this time and why he's been a pain in the neck to you. Kind of makes sense. His mother didn't want him and he thought you and Joe didn't want him. At least you know where you're going now."

"Kelly, you're always the optimist. Do you ever see the glass half-empty? Don't answer. I know you don't, but that's why everyone loves you. Do you know a good family counselor in the area? Think I'd better go out of town for this. Sure enough, if we even went to the one in town once, someone would see us and everyone would know in minutes. Wade doesn't need that now. He's got enough to deal with."

"So do you, my friend. Yes, there's a man who comes to the coffee shop from time to time. He lives up in Sunset Bay. He gave me his card once. Here it is." She gave Roxie his name and telephone number. "Tell him I referred you. He seems like a good man. Well, spend some time with your stepson and try and relax. You've had a stressful day. Do you need to take a little time off? If you do, I can get someone to cover for you."

"No. I think that might make Wade feel there was something really wrong with him if I had to stay home from work. I'll see you tomorrow morning, and Kelly, thanks for being my friend and so understanding."

"Roxie, I'm always here for you. You know I believe that family comes first. See you tomorrow."

She hung up and sat for a few minutes, digesting what Roxie had told her.

Well, guess this means that Jeff Black isn't a threat to me or Rebel at the moment now that he's in jail. Wonder if Amber knew about the marijuana farm on the back of the property? If Jeff fired his guard for selling marijuana to someone and was afraid they would find out it was from his farm, who knows what he might do to someone to keep the authorities from finding out about it.

CHAPTER SIXTEEN

Kelly had just begun to water the neglected plants on her deck when she heard her phone ring. She laid the hose down and went inside. "This is Kelly." She listened for a moment. "Hi, Mike. Heard from Roxie that you did a wonderful thing for her family today. Sounds like the fire was really something." She paused. "I'll see what I can come up with. See you in a few."

Well, so much for the plants and the house. Oh well, think it was Scarlett O'Hara who said "tomorrow is another day." Tomorrow I'll clean the house and finish the watering. Now I need to fix some dinner for Mike, but I've got to turn off the hose or it'll flood the deck.

She walked out onto the deck to turn off the hose. Rebel had never been a dog that chewed up furniture or anything else like that, but there was something about a garden hose he couldn't resist. He had the hose in his mouth, shaking both his head and the hose. Water had sprayed all over the deck.

"Well, Rebel, looks like you did a better job watering the plants than I did. Inside, boy."

A few minutes later Mike knocked on her door and then let himself in. Mike looked about as tired as she'd ever seen him.

"Welcome, Mr. Sheriff," she said with a smile. "You look like you need a friend and some food."

He kissed her lightly on the cheek. "At the moment I would welcome both along with a glass of wine. This has been some day."

She poured him a cold glass of Chardonnay and said, "Mike, before you start telling me about the Black's ranch, I need to tell you something and you may not be too happy about it."

Kelly told him about her trip out to Doc's ranch, starting from when she'd left the coffee shop and ending when she'd pulled out of Doc's driveway, leaving nothing out.

"Why didn't you tell me you were planning to do something like that? It could have been very dangerous for you and still might be."

"Well, Mike, for one thing, it was kind of a spur-of-the-moment thing. For another, I knew you wouldn't want me to do it, and I didn't want to get in an argument with you."

He frowned and was quiet for several moments. "Kelly, do you know the danger you could be in?"

"Mike, Doc is a really nice guy. Life hasn't been particularly kind to him. Maybe I'm being naïve, but I believe him. He told me everything, even though he didn't have to. I think he trusts me."

"You realize now you know everything there is to know about Doc and all about his past. If Doc is the killer, what makes you think the same thing won't happen to you that happened to Amber?"

"You're overreacting. I'm sure Doc didn't do it."

"Glad you are. I'm not. He had a motive for doing it – a very powerful motive – keeping his past secret and not having his cover completely blown. The autopsy showed that Amber was pregnant, not that she'd had an abortion, so obviously he didn't make that mistake again. However, he's just gone to the top of my list of suspects."

"What are you talking about? I thought Jeff Black was high on your list, although if he's in jail, he's probably pretty harmless at the moment."

"I had a long talk with Brandon after I arrested his father and took him to jail. I went back to the ranch and asked Brandon if Amber knew about the pot being grown on the ranch. He was very emphatic and said she didn't have a clue. He was so ashamed of it, he'd never told anyone. He told me Amber claimed she hated drugs. Evidently her cousin, Ginger's sister's child, died from a drug overdose. She'd started out using pot and kept going up the drug chain ladder until she overdosed on heroin. It seems to be pretty popular with young people right now. He told me how much Jeff liked Amber and that he'd even told Brandon that if the two of them got married, Jeff would buy them a ranch of their own. He certainly could be the killer, but I think Doc has a stronger motive."

"Can't say I feel the same way. Jeff's still pretty high on my list of suspects. How's Brandon doing?"

"Better than I would have expected, but Marcy is not doing well at all. She was packing her clothes while I was there. She's leaving Jeff and taking Brandon with her to her sister's home in Portland. She told Brandon they would come back to Cedar Bay so he could deliver the valedictorian speech, but she wouldn't stay in the ranch house and she wouldn't see Jeff. She was on the phone with an attorney when I left and from what I overheard, it had nothing to do with posting bail for Jeff. Poor Brandon. First Amber, then the fire, his parent's headed for divorce, and now being uprooted from the only home he's ever known. I hope he'll be okay in college. That's a lot of emotional stuff for anyone to deal with. He's had too many changes in his young life, but I can understand how Marcy feels."

"Do you think she knew Jeff was growing marijuana?"

"I don't know how she could not know. The smell alone would have alerted her that something was going on. If Brandon knew, I find it hard to believe that Marcy didn't, but it really doesn't make any difference. The ranch is solely in his name. The only thing she's done is live on a property where marijuana was being grown and that's not a crime. If she did know, I imagine she's going to spend a lot of sleepless nights thinking about the damage the crop that was grown on her husband's ranch might have done to a lot of people. Brandon remembered a dinner conversation one evening between his mother and Amber. They were talking about the fact that marijuana was being legalized in so many states and they both were very opposed to marijuana becoming legal."

"Well, if she said that, you wouldn't think she knew about what was being grown on the property."

"Aah, Kelly. One of the reasons I love you is that you like to believe people are basically good. Think about it. Money buys a lot of nice things and Marcy likes nice things, particularly jewelry. Just because she said that to Amber doesn't mean she didn't know about it. It may have been a lot easier to look the other way and take the things the money from the crops could get her. Anyway, that's what's happening out at the ranch. I have one more troubling thing to tell you."

"Swell. I'm not sure I can take much more. Okay, tell me what it is."

"I got a call from Seth Morrison, the computer guy. Chris took his computer into the shop Saturday, before the funeral. He told Chris it was frozen and he couldn't get it to work. Seth told him he couldn't look at it right then because he had several others he had to fix first. He finally was able to get to it yesterday afternoon. He decided to see if the problem was on the hard drive. When he opened the hard drive he found a number of child pornography sites on it. He pulled up a couple and given Amber's death, thought I should know. This, coupled with what I'd already found out about his previous activities makes Chris a suspect in my book."

"Great. The list just keeps growing. Can you arrest him for something like having child pornography on his computer?"

"Technically I could since Seth told me he found some child

pornography on it, but I've decided not to arrest him. I'd rather hold off and see if he's Amber's killer. So that makes three suspects, Jeff, Doc and Chris. And I'd have to add Brandon to that list. We don't know for sure that he didn't kill her. That makes four suspects. To change the subject, have you ever been on Chris's boat?"

"No, why?"

"If Chris killed Amber, he'd have to get her body in the water without being seen. I can't believe someone wouldn't have seen him if he just dropped her overboard from his boat. The autopsy showed she was murdered early in the morning. I wonder if he has a rowboat."

"If he did it, do you think he used a rowboat to dispose of Amber's body? I remember talking to him a few months ago, kidding him about how he stayed in such good shape because his boat was too small to have much exercise equipment on board. He mentioned something about rowing every morning when he got up. Said it was the best exercise he'd ever found, plus he liked the peace and quiet on the water early in the morning."

"Hmm. That would certainly be one way to dispose of a body. Think I need to pay him a visit and take a look at his boating set up."

"Mike, I know you didn't say it, but are you thinking that if Chris is the killer, he's also Amber's mystery man? I guess I can answer my own question. If he's the mystery man and the father of her child, can you imagine what the townspeople would have thought? If Amber had lived they probably would have rallied around Brandon if it turned out Brandon was the father. But Chris? I think they'd have his head on a platter. Having Amber's English teacher and the football coach father her child when everyone knows that she and Brandon were very serious about each other? Tongues would wag for months over that one.

"And if that's true, Chris would have a powerful motive for killing Amber," Kelly said. "He's already been fired from one school district for putting pictures of himself and an underage girl on a child pornography site. If nothing else, he would have been fired by our school district for having sex with a minor. Good grief, what a mess. And we're still no closer to finding out who did it. I wonder who else has a motive? Got anyone in mind?"

"No. I think it will all come to a head in the next few days. Meanwhile, how about fixing me some dinner? The county fire chief called me as soon as the fire broke out at three this morning and I'm whipped. Hate to eat and run, but don't think I'd be much company tonight."

"Kelly," Mike said when he finished eating, "I don't know how you work your magic, but I always feel so much better when I'm with you, to say nothing of how great my stomach feels. Who else can make a stuffed pork loin on a moment's notice with fresh green beans and a strawberry tart? Ummm. At the moment, this happy man is going home and sleep. I'll give you a call tomorrow. Thanks for being here for me."

"Mike, please believe me when I say I love making your life easier. And when you're a cook and someone loves your food, you just keep wanting to do more for them. Go now, or I might ask you to stay and as relaxed as you are at the moment, you might just do it."

CHAPTER SEVENTEEN

"Rebel, we've got some work to do. I've got to deliver some breakfast goodies to the yacht club for the meeting tomorrow morning. As long as I'm going to be at the marina, I'm going to wrap up the last of the strawberry tart and we're going to pay someone a visit."

Ten minutes later she parked her minivan in the parking lot next to the pier. Adjacent to the pier was a small marina owned by the county. The marina consisted of a floating dock and boat slips for approximately thirty boats. Private boat owners leased the boat slips from the county for a nominal sum. Kelly walked down the gangway that led to the dock and started looking for Chris's boat.

From the conversations she'd had with Chris over the last few months, she had a pretty good idea of where his boat slip was located. He'd told her he had a 35' sailboat and that it had a teak deck which required a lot of upkeep. He'd also mentioned it was located on the end of the dock. She looked at the row of boats and there, at the end of the dock, she saw it.

"C'mon Rebel. Let's deliver this strawberry tart to Chris."

She stepped on the boat's gunwale, walked around to the rear of the boat, and knocked on the sliding glass door to let Chris know someone was aboard. She saw him sitting on a leather couch, reading, and waved to him when he looked up. He walked over to the sliding door and opened it for them. "Kelly, Rebel, this is a surprise. Please, come in. What's the occasion for the visit?"

"Well," she said. "I had to deliver a coffee cake and a French toast casserole to the yacht club for their monthly business meeting tomorrow morning. Since I was coming down here and I had a leftover piece of one of your favorites in my refrigerator, I thought I'd drop it off. Here." She handed him the tart. "Enjoy!"

"Thanks. I'll have it as a late dessert. Funny you should mention the yacht club. Every time I walk up the gangway and see that dilapidated old building they call a yacht club, I have to laugh to myself. I'm surprised they have enough money to pay you to fix something for them."

"Chris, that club has been around longer than I have. The members pay just enough to keep it open. I've been preparing breakfast snacks for their monthly business meetings for years. I can't believe they have much business to discuss. I think it's more a matter of having a reason to get together."

"Well, from the bar business they do in the evening, I don't think having a reason to get together is a problem. Probably a good thing they don't have a restaurant in there or I'd hear them all night. As it is, it's pretty lively around the cocktail hour."

"So I hear. By the way, I have a view of the bay from my house and from the few lights I see on the boats at night, there must not be many people living on them."

"That's true. The marina holds thirty boats and out of those there are only three or four of us who live aboard. I love everything about the ocean. I love the smell, the water lapping against the sides of the boat, and the way the ocean rocks me to sleep at night. It never fails to work for me. Let me show her to you."

She followed him while he showed her how he could convert the kitchen counter into a dining table and the compactness of the bathroom and his bedroom. It was one of the most tastefully done interiors she had ever seen. She marveled at how efficient everything was on the boat.

"Chris, this is beautiful. You'd mentioned that the teak deck required a lot of upkeep. Looks like the interior does as well."

"Yes. This is an old boat. I don't think they make them like this anymore. It's my home and my hobby. Everything I need is here. I never wanted to be tied to mowing the lawn and all the other stuff that goes with having a traditional home. I wish I had time to take her out more. Teaching and coaching as well as all the other obligations I have at school don't allow me to have much free time, but occasionally I make time to take her out for a sail."

"Chris, your boat is one of the most inviting homes I've ever seen. The dark wood paneling, the leather couch and chair, everything. Not only is the exterior of the boat beautiful, the interior is just as beautiful. I couldn't see the name on the boat when I walked up. What do you call her?"

"I named her Avalon. Being an English teacher, I'm a big King Arthur fan. According to Arthurian legend, it was the island where King Arthur's sword Excalibur was forged. In the more modern context, it means a one-of-a-kind woman. Since boats are always referred to as 'she,' I thought the name was perfect for a one-of-a-kind boat."

"Beautiful. I love it. Thanks for sharing her story with me. I remember you telling me once that you rowed every morning. I assume you do it in the dinghy I saw tied to the side of the boat. Do you go to the same place every morning?"

"Pretty much. I don't like to go too far out in the dinghy. It doesn't have a motor and while I'm pretty good at rowing, I don't want to be out in the open ocean in a storm, so I'm usually within a couple of hundred yards from shore. I go south one day and north the next to break it up, but with Mother Nature being like she is, no two days are alike. I've seen incredible sights – whales, seals, eagles –

and those are just a few!"

"Well, from the exercise weights I see over in the corner, it looks like rowing isn't your only form of exercise," Kelly said, a worried look appearing on her face. She started to walk over to them, remembering that the burlap bag found with Amber's body had free weights in it.

Chris picked up on the change in her attitude, stepped in front of her and said, "Kelly, thanks for bringing the tart to me. I'd love you to stay and talk, but we both have to get up early. I'll see you at the usual time tomorrow," he said opening the sliding glass door for her. She and Rebel had no choice but to walk through it.

Well now, that's interesting. He's certainly moved to the top of my suspect list. Free weights, a dinghy, and a man who could easily row a boat out several hundred yards and drop a body over the side. Hmmm. Think I better call Mike when I get home.

*****

"Mike, I'm glad you answered. Chris has just gone to the top of my suspect list."

"Your suspect list?" he asked, emphasizing the word "your." "In case you've forgotten, and you seem to have, I'm the county sheriff and you are the owner of Kelly's Koffee Shop. What have you done now?"

"Well, after you left, I got to thinking."

He interrupted her. "That's dangerous. Whenever you say that, I get nervous."

She was glad she was talking to him on the phone because he probably wouldn't have appreciated the dirty look she gave him via the phone. "Anyway, I remembered that Chris told me he got his exercise every morning from rowing his dinghy in the ocean. I had to deliver a couple of things to the yacht club for their monthly business meeting tomorrow morning, so I thought I'd take him a leftover piece of strawberry tart. I know it's one of his favorites. You know, the one you like so much."

"Kelly," he interrupted, "I'm not interested in the strawberry tart right now. What did you find out?"

"I'm going to overlook the tone of your voice and chalk it up to your being tired."

"I'm sorry I snapped and I am tired. So what did you find out?"

"His boat is beautiful and I saw the dinghy he owns. He rows it every morning a few hundred yards from shore. He also had some free weights in a corner of the boat."

"Free weights? Are you sure? That's really interesting. You do remember, don't you, that Amber's body was weighted down with them. And someone who rows every morning probably wouldn't attract any attention when they took their boat out. He's strong enough he could easily lift her body into his dinghy and then drop it overboard when he was out of sight. Do you think he had any idea why you were there?"

"Not at first, but when I tried to look at the weights he quickly ushered me off the boat. I don't know if he suspects anything, but his attitude changed from being very friendly to almost icy."

"Kelly, Kelly, what am I going to do with you? I know Rebel is protective, but I'm getting really worried about you. Now it looks like there are four suspects, all of whom might like to see you deep-sixed. Actually, I've just made an executive decision. I'm going to be spending the nights at your house until this thing is solved. I know Rebel is a great guard dog, but I'd feel better if I was there. Maybe between both of us, we can keep you safe, because you certainly seem incapable of doing it yourself. I'll be there in a few minutes." He ended the call before she could say anything.

A few minutes later she opened the door for him. "Mike, I'm

sorry for worrying you, but if it means you're going to spend more time here, then it's worth it. Come in, it's getting late and we both need some sleep, but that doesn't mean we have to go to sleep immediately once we get in bed," she said with a twinkle in her eyes and a smile on her face.

CHAPTER EIGHTEEN

Kelly swung her long legs over the side of the bed and got out as quietly as possible so she wouldn't wake Mike up. She let Rebel out, fed him, and got dressed. Minutes later they left for the coffee shop.

It was another busy morning at Kelly's. Everyone wanted to talk about what had happened at the Black's ranch and what was going to happen to Jeff Black. The gossipmongers were more than happy to share their tidbits, the biggest of which seemed to be that Marcy and Brandon had left Cedar Bay yesterday afternoon.

Someone claimed that Marcy had called the principal and told him Brandon would be able to deliver the valedictorian speech, but that he would not be attending classes during this last week of school. The principal said he understood and it wouldn't affect Brandon's class standing or grade average, because the last week of school for seniors was more or less a time for saying goodbye to each other, signing yearbooks, and taking pictures, rather than furthering their education. Everyone felt sorry for Brandon.

Speculation at the coffee shop was also high on whether or not Marcy would actually leave Jeff permanently. Some hinted that Marcy probably had several male friends in surrounding towns and that the only reason she had stayed with Jeff was for the money. No one knew if Jeff had other assets or hidden money, but there was talk that if he did, Marcy would probably return.

When Kelly walked into the storage room to get more napkins and silverware during the lunch hour she noticed she had a message on her phone from Amber's best friend, Lindsay Williams, asking her to call. Even though there were a number of customers who were ready to order, she decided to return the call.

"Thanks for getting back to me, Mrs. Conner. If you have some time after the coffee shop closes today, I was wondering if I could stop by. I'd like to talk to you."

"Why don't you come here about three this afternoon? I should be finished with everything by then. Want to tell me what this is about?"

"No, I don't know if it's important, but it's been bothering me ever since Amber died."

"Okay. See you then."

Promptly at three there was a timid knock on the front door of the coffee shop. Kelly walked over to it and saw Lindsay standing outside. "Come in. Would you like some iced tea or a soft drink?"

"No thanks," she said in a shaky voice as she stood in front of Kelly.

"Why don't we sit in a booth? I think they're a little more comfortable. I'll be with you in a minute. I need a refill for my iced tea." She knew she'd probably had enough caffeine for the day, but she wanted to give Lindsay a moment or two to compose herself.

When she returned to the booth she said, "I can see this is difficult for you, Lindsay. What can I do to help?"

Lindsay began to cry softly. "I don't know where to start. It just hurts so much, knowing I'll never see Amber again." Tears slid down her face. Kelly stepped behind the counter, got a box of Kleenex, and set it on the table in front of Lindsay. Lindsay took several out and tried to wipe away her tears.

"Mrs. Conner, I know Amber really liked you. I know you and the county sheriff are close. I've been debating whether I should tell him this, but I was afraid he might think it was just silly girl stuff."

"Lindsay, I promise you I won't think whatever you tell me is silly girl stuff, okay?"

"Thank you." She shuddered, took a deep breath, and began to speak. "I've known Amber for as long as I can remember. She was my best friend. We did everything together from talk about boys to go to church together to becoming cheerleaders, everything. I knew her better than anyone else in the world. I think I knew her even better than her parents did."

"Yes, I often heard Amber speak about you. It was evident from the way she spoke about you that you were her best friend."

"Well, here's the thing. I know you hired Madison to work here, but I don't know if you really know what went on between her and Amber."

"She told me she and Amber didn't get along."

Lindsay laughed bitterly. "That's putting it mildly. Madison hated Amber. It started last fall. Madison and Brandon had gone out together a few times. One night after football practice when we'd been practicing our cheerleading routines at their scrimmage, Amber couldn't get her old car started. She tried several times. Nothing happened. Brandon was walking to his car and offered to help. He tried to get it started and again, nothing. He offered to take Amber home. From what Amber told me the next morning they sat in his car and talked for two hours. He never took Madison out again and he and Amber started going steady. They were voted homecoming king and homecoming queen. There's no doubt they were the most popular couple in school.

"Everyone was so happy for them when they both got scholarships to Oregon State. It was kind of like if you were near the golden couple, you were golden too. There was only one person who wasn't happy about it. That was Madison. You probably know she comes from a bad background. Her father's a washed-up fisherman who's never had a real job. He even tried to start an oyster farm business, but it failed too. He's a real loser.

"Her mother left them when Madison was a little girl. The only thing positive Madison ever did was go out with Brandon, the star quarterback, a few times. When she was with him, for the first time in her life, she felt like she was someone. I don't know if you know about her grades, but she barely got the grade point average she needed to have to graduate. Believe me, it was that close.

"Anyway, after Brandon stopped seeing her, Madison began to hate Amber. I mean really hate her. I can't begin to tell you how many bad things she did to make Amber's life miserable. Amber would turn in a finished essay or test to a teacher and it would disappear. Her locker was broken into and nude photographs were put in it. Everything was stolen out of it - her cheerleading sweater, some personal things, her purse with her wallet which had her driver's license in it. After the homecoming dance, she found the sash she'd worn cut into pieces and scattered outside the front door of the school. It was one thing after another. Amber finally figured out who was doing these things against her and told the principal. He called Madison into his office and told her if there was one more incident, she would be expelled from school.

"Was Amber afraid of Madison?" Kelly asked.

"That's what I'm getting to. Yes. A few weeks ago Amber was walking to her car. She'd stayed at school later than usual to help tutor a freshman who was having trouble with algebra. No one was around. As Amber was getting into her car Madison walked up to her and threatened her."

"What do you mean, threatened her? Did Amber tell you exactly what she said?" Kelly asked.

"Yes, Madison said 'You better watch out. You ruined my life and took Brandon away from me. I'm going to kill you.' That's exactly what Amber told me she'd said to her. I'll never forget those words and now with what's happened…"

Kelly reached across the table and put her hands over Lindsay's. "Oh Lindsay, you poor thing. Have you told this to anyone else?"

"No. I'm not sure they'd believe me. It's a pretty common thing in high school for girls to hate one another. That's why I didn't go to the sheriff. Like I told you earlier, I was afraid he'd think it was stupid girl stuff."

"Well, since you came here and told me, you obviously don't think it's stupid girl stuff and neither do I. Let me ask you this. From both a physical and psychological standpoint, do you think that Madison, because of her hatred of Amber, was capable of killing Amber?"

Lindsay sat quietly for a few moments with her head bowed, looking down at the table, obviously deep in thought. Finally, she raised her head and looked directly at Kelly. "Mrs. Conner, I've asked myself that question a million times in the last few days and I think the answer is yes. She's physically very strong. I know she works out a lot with weights. Hate to say it, but sometimes when someone doesn't have much in the brain department, they try to make up for it in the body department. You know what I mean?"

"Psychologically, who knows? She sure hasn't had much parenting. I've heard her dad drinks a lot and when he gets drunk, he's a mean drunk. I even heard that he'd hit Madison a couple of times. It wouldn't surprise me because she's come to school with bruises a bunch of times and once she even had a black eye. She had to use a lot of make-up to cover it. I remember because it was the day the cheerleader photographs were taken for the yearbook and we all wanted to look really good. She said she'd missed a step on some stairs and fell down. I always thought that was strange. She basically kind of raised herself. She's never had any friends. I think the only reason Brandon went out with her a few times is because of you know."

"No. What do you mean?" asked Kelly.

"Well, all the guys knew Madison was easy. They liked to brag that she had 'hinges on her heels.' There was even a rumor that they used to pass her around after the football games. She and Brandon really didn't go together. He was more of a gentleman than a lot of the other guys. I think he felt like he should take her out before he had sex with her. Anyway, in her mind it meant they were going together, but they weren't. I think she was so desperate for attention that when the star quarterback paid some attention to her, she fantasized that it was more than it really was."

"Lindsay, I can't even imagine how hard this must have been for you to come here and talk to me. Thanks for trusting me. Do you have any objection to my telling Mike about our conversation? I think it's very important and should be part of his investigation."

"No. If you think it might help find who killed Amber, tell him whatever you want. I know it will never bring her back, but something is totally off with Madison."

"Lindsay, you need to go home. This has been very emotional for you. Try and get some rest. You need to be fresh for graduation and by the way, your singing is absolutely beautiful. I was amazed that you could do as well as you did at your best friend's funeral. That must have been very hard for you. Do you plan on pursuing singing as a career?"

"Well, I'm lucky I was able to get a scholarship to a small college in Washington that specializes in music, so sure, I'm hoping I can, but let me tell you, singing at Amber's funeral was the hardest thing I've ever had to do."

"I'm sure college and your music career will work out well for you. And Lindsay, Madison may work for me, but I promise you that she will never know about this conversation."

"Believe me, Mrs. Conner, it's a conversation I wish I never had to have. Thanks for listening."

Kelly closed the door and locked it when Lindsay left, glad to be alone. Rebel sensed her sadness and looked up at her with his big brown eyes.

"Rebel, I don't know what to think. Here's another suspect with a motive for killing Amber. That makes five. I'm sure Mike will have some thoughts on it. Let's go home, big guy."

CHAPTER NINETEEN

It was early evening and Kelly had just finished watering the plants and cleaning the bathroom and kitchen when she heard Mike knock, unlock the front door, and open it.

"I like the sound of you opening the door. It seems pretty natural," she said, walking over to Mike and giving him a big hug.

"Well, I have to admit I like knowing someone is waiting for me and that I'll probably get a pretty good dinner. Speaking of which, what is it tonight? I know it's early, but I'd like to start thinking about it."

"Tonight we're having my famous meat loaf, mashed potatoes, and asparagus. I made a lot, figuring I could take the rest to the coffee shop and make meat loaf sandwiches tomorrow for the lunch crowd."

"Good planning. I stopped by my place and picked up some clothes. Let me put them away and I'll be back in a few minutes."

"Okay, Kelly," he said as he walked down the hall into the kitchen. "What kind of trouble did you get into today?"

"No trouble, Mike, but I did have an interesting conversation with Amber's best friend, Lindsay Williams. She wanted to talk to you, but thought you might dismiss what she had to say as silly girl stuff, so she called and asked if she could come by the coffee shop and talk to me. I was surprised to hear what she had to say. I think it might be important to your investigation. We'd heard that Madison hated

Amber, but I'd kind of dismissed it. According to Lindsay, Madison really hated Amber, far more than I knew."

Mike opened the refrigerator and took out a beer. "Okay, shoot. What did she have to say?" Kelly sat across from him at the kitchen table and related the details of her conversation with Lindsay. When she was finished, he sat quietly, deep in thought.

He took a sip of his beer. "I'm not sure I've ever had a case with this many possible suspects. You've done a lot of the work for me and you've talked to all of the possible suspects. What's your take? Who do you think did it?"

"I'm frustrated. In my mind there had been four solid suspects and now I have to add Madison. That makes five. I know there's a possibility that Jeff did it, but my intuition tells me no, however I could be wrong. He certainly had a motive if he thought Amber knew about the marijuana farm he had and he was worried she would tell someone."

"Kelly, I'm not ruling him out. He's definitely still a suspect in my book, even if he is in the county jail. Looks like he'll get out on bail tomorrow."

"The next one is Doc. He had a reason to kill her, actually a very good reason. He's trying to make a new life and doesn't want his cover blown. What if he didn't tell me everything? All we know is pretty much what you were able to find out about him and what he told me. He befriended Amber and she talked to him about getting an abortion. But what if there's more? Maybe she knew something about him that he didn't tell me. I don't know, but having your cover blown might be motive enough."

"I agree, Kelly. The thing that bothers me is that Amber was drowned. To my knowledge, I don't think Doc has a boat, but maybe he keeps one somewhere on his property. Did you see any kind of a small motorboat, perhaps on a trailer, when you were out there?"

"No," Kelly said. "Doc's place was spotless. You know how lots of people who own small ranches often have junk piled up all around their house. You could eat off the ground around his place. There wasn't a bit of trash. He takes as much care of the outside of his house as he does the inside. Call it instinct, but I don't think he did it." She paused for a moment. "Then again, I didn't go in his garage. Maybe he has a boat in there."

"Well, if he has a boat, he'd probably be the top suspect on my list, but from what we know, I can't connect the dots without a boat."

"Let's talk about Madison. Her dad's fished the bay forever and has a small boat. I would imagine she's been out in that boat a number of times and is probably pretty familiar with the coastline and the bay. She's strong and she certainly had a motive for killing Amber, even if it was all in her mind. Don't forget, according to Lindsay, Madison threatened to kill Amber."

"Maybe I'm naïve," Mike said, "but I can't imagine that a young woman would kill another young woman out of jealousy and that's primarily what her motive would have been."

"I agree. She certainly has led a tough life, but I haven't seen anything that makes me think she's unbalanced. Lindsay says she's not very smart and is barely going to be able to graduate. There's nothing that would point to Amber's death being premeditated and it would require some brains to think to weight a body down and dump it in the ocean. Maybe I just hate to think she was the one who did it, but that doesn't keep her from being a suspect. I wonder if she was in her first class on the morning Amber was murdered. According to Ginger, Amber left the house at 5:00 a.m. It seems hard for me to believe that Madison could have killed Amber and then gone to school as if nothing had happened."

"I'll call the principal in the morning and find out if she was in school that morning," Mike said.

Kelly went on, "Then there's Chris. He rows his boat every morning, is knowledge about the ocean, and owns some free weights, so he certainly qualifies as a suspect. What I'm struggling with is his motive. I've never heard anything that remotely gives him a reason to kill her."

"Well don't forget we still don't know who the mystery man is that Amber referred to in her diary, someone she was having a sexual relationship with," Mike said. "Maybe Amber was flirting with him at school. It's not that unusual for a young high school girl to become infatuated with her teacher. She could have been teasing him by wearing too short of a skirt or giving him a peek down her blouse or something like that. Maybe Chris takes the bait, one thing leads to another, and suddenly Amber tells him she's pregnant."

"That would sure give him a reason to kill her. Mike, we haven't even talked much about the fifth suspect, Brandon. What if he was the one Amber was going to tell about the pregnancy and he was afraid it would ruin his chances to play football for Oregon State? Or what if he found out Amber was seeing someone else and was jealous? We've said jealousy would have provided a motive for Madison. Well, the same thing applies to Brandon, maybe even more so. Even though everyone feels sorry for him, he, too, has to be a real suspect. When you call the principal, see if Brandon was in his first class that morning."

"Kelly, those are the five we have so far. Hopefully, no more suspects will turn up. At least we've solidly identified five people who each have a powerful motive to kill Amber. Wouldn't have thought it was possible a couple of weeks ago. I do now."

"Mike, we're starting to go around in circles. I'm going to let all of this settle in my subconscious. I'm not having much luck solving it consciously. Time to eat. It's been another long day for both of us."

CHAPTER TWENTY

The next afternoon after everyone, including Roxie and Charlie, had left the coffee shop for the day, Madison turned to Kelly. "Do you have time to talk to me?" she asked.

"Of course. Let's get some iced tea and sit down. We could both stand to get off of our feet."

"Okay, Madison. I'm all yours. Finally it's quiet in here. What did you want to talk to me about?"

"I know this is gonna sound kinda strange, but I've been talkin' to Father Brown."

Kelly raised an eyebrow. "Really, what about?"

Madison went on, "I told you I really felt good after bein' in church at Amber's funeral. My dad's an atheist and he never took me to church. You probably know my mother left us when I was very young. My childhood hasn't been the easiest. I see all these lovin' families and something inside me hurts so bad sometimes I can hardly stand it. I'd give anything to be part of a happy lovin' family, but it just never happened."

She took a deep breath and continued. "I've never told anyone this, but I feel I can tell you because you've been kind of like a mother to me these past few days. My dad drinks and he's a mean drunk. I can usually tell when he's been drinkin' and I make a point to keep out of his way. A coupla times I was asleep when he came home and he woke me up, really angry with me." She turned away from Kelly.

"When he gets angry he hits things, like me. I've never felt loved. My mother left me. My dad's a drunk. I really don't have any friends. The reason I'm tellin' you this is that when I was in church I felt loved for the first time in my life. God's love, maybe, I dunno. It just kinda overwhelmed me. It was the strangest thing. The afternoon of the funeral after I finished up here I went back to the church and sat inside on one of the pews for a long time. I felt somethin' while I was sitting there that I've never felt before, kind of a wonderful peaceful feelin'. Anyway, Father Brown walked in and came over to me. He sat next to me for a long time and didn't say nothin'. Finally, he reached over and took my hand and said he'd like to help me. I don't know why he did that. Maybe he knew about my father or maybe it was somethin' in the way my face looked. I started cryin' and couldn't talk. He led me to his office in the back of the church and told me he was there for me. He said if I'd like to talk, he was happy to listen."

"He's a wonderful man. You couldn't have found anyone better to confide in. I'm glad he was there for you."

Tears welled up in Madison's eyes. "I talked to him for over two hours. I told him about my childhood, my dad, my mother leavin', everything. I told him I'd done some bad things to Amber and I hated myself for doin' them, but I was so jealous of her I couldn't help myself. I told him I wanted to feel peaceful all the time, like I did when I was in his church. He told me I was one of God's children. Comin' from anyone else it would have sounded pretty corny, but comin' from him it meant a lot to me. For the first time in my life, I began to hope that maybe I could be happy and peaceful."

"Does that mean you're going to join the Catholic Church?" Kelly asked.

"Yes. I've met with him two more times and he said he'd prepare me for becomin' a Catholic. He tol' me I needed to get a sponsor and I thought of you. Kelly, would you be my sponsor?"

"Oh, honey, it would be my honor. I'm so glad that Amber's death led to something positive for someone."

"You know it's funny. He told me that the things I tol' him, you know, my sins, weren't no worse than anyone else's. I guess maybe I ain't such a bad person after all. I really think this is a turnin' point for me. Who knows? Jes' might be able to earn enough money to go to cosmetology school. Always loved playin' around with hair and make-up. There's one up in Sunset Bay. Maybe if I earn enough money this summer, and if you'd let me work here in the fall, I might be able to do it. I really think this is just the beginnin' of my life. I'm pretty excited."

"I'm pretty excited for you too, Madison. We'll make it work. Why don't you apply to that school? If you need some money for tuition, I could probably make you a loan against your future pay. If you need a recommendation, you can use me. I could also say a few words to Wanda, who owns the beauty shop here in town. She told me the other day that Missy was planning to retire next year. It seems that the timing would be right. She said she'd be looking for someone. Maybe you could help her in the shop until you get your license."

"Kelly, I can never thank you enough for being so understandin' and helpin' me. For the first time in my life, I feel really, really good."

"Madison, maybe you should think about moving in with someone, renting a room or something. I really don't like to think of you living with your father."

"I think I need to tell him that I'm joinin' the church. Maybe if he knows that I'll be confessin' my sins weekly, he might be afraid that I'll say somethin' about him."

"Be careful. You might want to think about calling me or Mike if it happens again. Since you haven't turned eighteen yet, maybe an arrest for child abuse would make him think twice about it. Any chance he'd agree to get some help for his drinking?"

"Don't think so. He's kind of private about a lot of things. He always apologizes to me afterwards and tells me he's sorry. I don't think he wants to do it. He can't help himself. I think he just turns into another person when he drinks, a person who's not very nice."

"All the more reason for him to get some help. Let me see what I can do. Now that you're starting a new life, sure would be great if you didn't have to deal with that problem. Do you have any relatives who live in the area?"

"No. There's no one. Just Dad and me." Madison looked at her watch and said, "Oops, I better get outta here. My first real meetin' with Father Brown is in fifteen minutes. I sure don't want to be late for that. Again, Kelly, thanks for everything."

"Not a problem. Tell Father Brown I'm really proud and honored to be your sponsor. Go." She opened the door and gave Madison a friendly push. "It's time to get on with your new life."

She had just closed the door and was getting ready to leave for the day when there was a knock on the door. "Yes, who is it?" she asked.

"It's Dottie, from the yacht club. I was driving by and saw Madison leave and figured you might still be here. I want to return the serving trays you brought by last night. The coffee cake and French toast casserole were great. There wasn't a crumb left. Here they are."

"Thanks, but I could have picked them up. What's this blue ribbon doing on top of the trays? I don't remember seeing it before."

"Of course you don't. I found it on the gangway this morning when I went down to our boat after the meeting. Our nephew's been living on it the last few months and I like to check in on him whenever I can. I remember cheerleaders wearing blue ribbons like this at the football games. I didn't want the ribbon to fall in the water, so I put it in the back seat of my car. Here, I'll take it."

"No, why don't I keep it? A lot of the cheerleaders' parents come in here and I'll see if it belongs to one of them."

"Well, if you don't mind. That's fine with me and it would save me a trip to the school. Looks like it got torn or something. I seem to remember them being much longer."

"Yes, it does look like something's happened to it. Thanks again for bringing these by."

"We were all talking this morning about your cheesecake. Any chance we could have that next month instead of something breakfasty? We all agreed it was crazy to have cheesecake at eight in the morning, but we decided we wouldn't tell anyone else about it."

"Not a problem. I'll plan on it. See you soon."

As soon as Dottie left, she took the blue ribbon from the top tray and examined it. She was certain it was the other half of the ribbon Amber had given to the "mystery man."

She finished her iced tea and washed the glass, thinking about the events of the last hour. *I never did feel that Madison was the one who killed Amber and after talking to her today, I'm more certain than ever. Sure, someone might feel guilty about what they'd done and turn to religion, but what sticks with me is that Father Brown told Madison her sins were no worse than anyone else's. I don't think she would lie about that, particularly now that I'm going to be her sponsor. She knows I could always ask Father Brown if he'd said that. He couldn't tell me what sins she may have confessed to him, but I'm sure he'd tell me if he said that her sins were no worse than anyone else's. I don't think Madison is a pathological liar or psychotic. I think she's a kid who's had a lousy home life. I hope everything works out for her. I just don't think she's the killer.*

And the blue ribbon? Sure could have come from Chris' boat. I don't think Doc did it, but maybe if I pay him another visit, I can find out a little more about him and see if he keeps a boat on the property.

"Come on, Rebel. Time to visit Doc again, but no filet mignon this time."

CHAPTER TWENTY-ONE

Kelly pulled into the driveway of Doc's ranch, opened the minivan door, and walked around to get Rebel out of the back seat. Doc was standing at the front door. "Kelly, two visits in one week. I must be pretty special. Come on in. What can I do for you?" he said, reaching down and scratching Rebel's ears.

"Doc, you know once you start that, he won't let you stop," she said laughing. "He might let you pause for a few minutes, but he'll definitely be back for more."

"Yeah, I know. I learned that early on at the coffee shop. He doesn't wag his tail at me for treats. He comes for scratches." He knelt down and looked Rebel in the eye. "I'm wise to you, boy."

"Doc, mind if we sit down? I'd like to talk very honestly with you."

"Of course not, Kelly. Shoot. What's so important that it couldn't wait until lunch tomorrow?"

"Doc, from what you told me about you and Amber a couple of days ago, you and I both know you could be a suspect in Amber's murder, but I just don't see you doing it. I know I might be in danger by coming here and talking to you if you murdered her, so I'm trusting my intuition by coming here today. I have a gut feeling you didn't tell me everything the other day."

"Kelly, I appreciate your trust in me. Let me reassure you I did not do it." He took a deep breath. "Okay, I'm going to be perfectly honest with you, just as you requested. Yes, I had a motive for killing her, but I didn't do it."

"Why don't you tell me what that motive might be? And if you didn't kill her, maybe I can figure out who did after we talk. I'd really like to eliminate you from the list of suspects."

"Believe me, that makes two of us." Doc swallowed several times and began, "What I told you the other day was the truth, but there's a little more to it. Amber came back to the ranch and paid me a visit for a second time a day later. She told me she'd thought about it a lot and she was pretty sure she wanted an abortion. She said she had to tell the father first and she was planning on doing that the next morning."

"Was that the morning she was murdered?"

"Yes. What I left out the other day was that although I was acquitted in the murder of the young woman in Southern California, a wrongful death lawsuit was filed against me by the girl's parents in civil court. I told you it was an election year and her father made sure that he got all the publicity he could from it. I was found liable in the lawsuit and the jury awarded the parents damages in the amount of three million dollars. I was afraid I would lose everything, all of my family antiques, the art, and everything else I'd inherited. I told you the truth about coming up here and starting a new life."

Well, that's interesting. Funny Mike's research never came up with any information about the civil lawsuit, Kelly thought.

"So they've never found you? Do you know if they're still looking for you?"

"The parents died in a plane crash a few months after the trial. They were flying in a private plane to a political event in Palm

Springs that was being held by a wealthy donor of his. According to what I learned on the Internet, apparently there was an engine malfunction. The pilot and the parents were killed instantly when the plane crashed into Mt. San Jacinto outside of Palm Springs. Even though the accident was investigated by the NTSB, they never could determine the exact cause of the accident. Fortunately, if anyone had found me, people in your coffee shop could swear that I had been in the coffee shop every day that week. After the parents died, their son received the right to collect the judgment against me, but he couldn't find me, and I think he's given up. I'd vanished only to wind up right here in Cedar Bay."

"What does that have to do with Amber?"

"I told you that I had told her about the criminal trial. Evidently she researched it on the Internet and discovered the information about the civil trial. I told her I wouldn't perform the abortion under any circumstances. I mean, think about it. Where would I do it? I told her the same thing and she said she was sure I could do it right here at the ranch. She threatened to expose me. She told me if I didn't perform the abortion once she'd decided to go through with it, she'd make sure that everything I owned would be seized by the court in order to pay the civil money judgment entered against me. She'd obviously done some research.

"You might be surprised if I told you these antiques and the artwork you see here in my home are probably worth a couple of million dollars. They mean everything to me and I don't want to lose them. I was desperately afraid she would carry out her threat and expose me."

"Good grief. That's a classic case of blackmail and certainly would provide you with a motive for killing Amber."

"I know that. I kicked myself after you were here the other day for having told you about my past. I knew I would be very high on the suspect list with a motive like that, but Kelly, you've got to believe me, I didn't do it."

"Doc, I never wanted to believe that you did do it. It never felt right to me. Let's think this through. The ocean played a part in her death. She was drowned in the bay. Do you have a boat?"

"Kelly, this is embarrassing, but I can't even swim. I'm scared to death of the ocean and I'd never consider owning a boat. I was a book nerd when I grew up. I went to college when I was sixteen and graduated in three years. Then I went to medical school and became one of the youngest medical doctors in California history. My whole life was about learning and my parents pushed me hard to become a doctor. No other career was an option for me from the time I started reading at a very early age. Physical exercise simply was not a part of my life. My parents never wanted me to participate in any sports because they were afraid I might be injured and wouldn't be able to become a doctor. Even something like swimming was off limits to me. You'll notice I'm probably the only person around here who doesn't have a horse. That's another thing I was never allowed to do – ride a horse."

"Doc, have you ever even been on a boat?"

"No. I not only have never been on a boat, but I would be terrified to be on one. I like things I can control. I can't control the ocean. It frightens me to even think about it."

"Well, it seems to me that whoever did this had a pretty good knowledge of the ocean. I mean if her body was pulled into shore, someone had to put her out there in the bay. From what you're telling me, that wouldn't be you."

"No, it certainly wouldn't. Kelly, you're not part of law enforcement. I know that you're close to the county sheriff, but why are you trying so hard to solve this case?"

"I'm Amber's godmother and her mother, Ginger, is my closest friend. I feel I have a responsibility to Amber and her mother to find out who did this."

"I didn't know that. Since you're not officially part of any law enforcement agency, can you tell me who else you suspect? Maybe I can help. Having treated so many people over the years, I'm a pretty good gauge of human nature."

"Okay. I've identified five suspects, all of whom have a motive for killing Amber. I've pretty much eliminated three of them and you would make the fourth." She told him her suspicions about Jeff. She said he was one of the three she had pretty much eliminated, but that she could be wrong. Next she described her recent conversation with Madison and why she didn't think she murdered Amber. Then she went on and told him that while Brandon might have had a motive, just as Madison and Jeff did, she didn't think he'd done it.

"I agree with your analysis of those people. I don't think any of three of them did it for the same reasons. If you eliminate me, that leaves one suspect. Want to tell me about him or her?"

"Doc, I hate to accuse anyone and I sure don't want to start a rumor, but I know you're very discrete. Here's what I think." She told him all the reasons she thought Chris was the murderer, concluding with the weights she'd seen on his boat. She also told him she thought Chris might suspect that she knew something and that Mike was concerned about her safety. "Actually, Doc, Mike insisted that he spend the nights at my home until this case is solved. He's worried I could be in danger. I reminded him Rebel was a guard dog, but he still insisted."

"I can see why, Kelly. It's pretty obvious to anyone who's seen Mike with you that he's crazy about you. I'm not at all surprised he's concerned. I would be too." He sat for several minutes thinking about what she'd said. "Back to Amber. In a normal case, we could compare Chris' DNA and the DNA of the unborn child, however, since Amber was cremated, that isn't possible. I suppose if he's nervous enough about being exposed, he'll do something to trip himself up, but we can't count on that."

"There's one other thing, Doc. I'll be back in a minute." She walked out to the old minivan. "Do you recognize this?" she asked when she returned, holding up the blue ribbon.

He took it from her hand and looked at it. "I think Amber used to wear one like this. What is it?"

"Pretty much a status symbol. The high school cheerleaders are given blue ribbons like this when they make the squad. They're really proud of them and they wear them all year. This one's too short. It looks like it was cut in half."

He ran his finger over the edge. "Yes, this definitely seems to have been cut or torn."

"Doc, there's something else I need to tell you. I found Amber's diary and read it. In it she referred to her pregnancy, a 'mystery man,' and her debate with herself over whether or not she should terminate the pregnancy. Here's the thing. She said that her 'mystery man' wanted a memento from her and she'd given him half of her blue ribbon. I'm certain this is it. It was given to me by a woman who was returning some trays to me at the coffee shop. I'd baked some things for the yacht club and she'd found it on the gangway when she went to her boat to see her nephew."

"Wow! With Chris living on his boat and using that gangway, if we could find his fingerprints on it, I would think it could be used as evidence."

"I don't know. Seems to me there would be so many fingerprints on it, it wouldn't stand up in court. Who knows how many people have touched it? And now both of our fingerprints are on it."

"Yeah, you're right. It's probably a good thing I never went into law enforcement. I didn't think of that."

"I wonder what Chris would say if I told him that Amber had confided in me and told me she was sure he was the father of her unborn child and she was debating what to do. I could tell him I suggested she should tell him and see what he said, that maybe he would want the baby and want to marry her."

"I don't think you should do that, Kelly. That seems awfully dangerous."

"I'd take Rebel with me. You know how protective he is of me. This can't go on much longer, Doc. And if he had nothing to do with it, I'm sure he'll have a plausible explanation for everything."

"Kelly, do me a favor. If you decide to do it, and I don't think it's a good idea, have Mike go with you. Might be a whole lot safer for you to have someone with you who has a gun. Remember, if it's Chris, he's already murdered once, so a second murder would probably seem much easier to him. Promise?"

"Okay," she said as she mentally crossed her fingers. "Doc, one other thing. Seems like a shame to waste your medical knowledge. Do you know much about alcohol abuse?"

"Of course. Like any doctor, a number of my patients were alcoholics. I'm very familiar with addiction. Why?"

"You know Madison, the young woman who replaced Amber at the coffee shop? The one I just told you I've pretty much eliminated as a suspect? Well, her father drinks too much and has even hit her when he's drunk. I was wondering if you could do something. I know you want to stay off the grid, but maybe it's time you became active in our town. Maybe you could do some counselling at the church or work with the psychologist in town as a volunteer. For some reason, I think maybe you could help him."

"Let me think about it. I kind of like my privacy, but I admit I am getting a little bored. Before you go, I need to give Rebel a treat." As soon as he heard the word 'treat,' Rebel got up and followed Doc into the kitchen. Kelly didn't even try to stop him. She was mentally planning how she was going to handle what might happen in the next hour.

"I'll see you tomorrow and I'll think about how I might be able to help Madison's father, but one of the main things in dealing with an alcoholic is getting them to admit they need help. Doesn't sound like he's quite there yet."

She kissed him on the cheek. "Doc, I knew you didn't do it. I just need to find out who did do it and right now I think we both know who that person is."

As soon as Kelly pulled out of the driveway, Doc called Mike. "Sheriff, this is Doc. I'm concerned that Kelly is going to do something really dangerous. She's been at my place for the last hour and told me everything she knows and I shared some things with her that I hadn't told her before. She and I are both pretty sure we know who the killer is and I'm afraid she's going to confront him by herself. She promised me she'd take you with her, but I've been around people long enough to know when they're lying to me, and I can almost guarantee you that she lied to me about that."

"Why was Kelly out at your place?" Mike asked in an angry tone of voice.

"She didn't think I was the killer and hoped her intuition was right. She told me she'd decided to confront me with what she knew and see what I said."

"That woman is driving me nuts," he said in an exasperated voice. "Okay, I'll wait until she gets home and talk to her about it."

"Hate to butt in, Sheriff, but I don't think I'd do that if I were you. I have a feeling there's no time to waste. I like Kelly and I want to help. How about if I meet you at your office as soon as I can get there? I'll fill you in then. I don't want to waste any more time on the phone. See you in a few minutes."

Before leaving to meet Mike, Doc walked into his bedroom and took his Glock nine millimeter pistol from the nightstand drawer where he kept it. He hadn't told Kelly, but even though he couldn't swim, and wasn't allowed to participate in any type of sport, his parents had insisted he become a crack marksman. They believed in the Second Amendment and had been lifelong members of the National Rifle Association. He tucked the pistol in his belt under the Pendleton shirt he wore. No one would be able to see it.

CHAPTER TWENTY-TWO

Rebel was so well-trained it was rare that Kelly ever put him on a leash unless it was some place that absolutely required it. She parked her minivan in its usual place not far from the coffee shop. She opened the door for Rebel and he jumped out and started towards the coffee shop. As usual, he was off leash.

"Not tonight, Rebel. This way." She motioned with her hand and walked down the marina gangway, the only sounds coming from the happy hour crowd at the yacht club. When she got to the bottom of the gangway, she was almost knocked into the water by a young man who rushed past her and ran up the gangway. She stood for a moment, trying to get her balance back then she looked back up the gangway to see if she knew who he was.

I don't recognize him. Wonder if he's from around here. I didn't see his face, but from the way he walks and carries himself, he looks like he's probably in his early 20's. Rebel stood next to her, guard hairs standing on end. She reached down and petted him.

"Hey, boy, easy. I'm okay." She heard a low rumbling sound coming from his chest. He stood next to her, looking at the back of the young man as he hurried into the parking lot. *That's so strange. Rebel's never done that before. Wonder what's up with him.*

"Come on Rebel. We've got work to do." She walked by several boats tied up to the floating dock, and had just turned down a finger of the dock that led to Chris's boat when Rebel stopped, blocking her path. He pushed at her legs with his strong body, making her back up and turn towards the second finger of the dock. He walked down it to the third boat and began growling again. Kelly had no choice but to follow him. "Rebel, what are you doing?" she whispered. "I don't want to be seen."

It was as if she hadn't even spoken. Rebel jumped onto the gunwale of the boat, continuing to growl. He looked back at her. "You want me to get on the boat? Is that what this is about?" she asked.

Kelly remembered his early days as a drug dog. *I wonder if he smells something on the boat. Maybe I should call Mike. Right! He'd tell me to get off the boat before someone shoots both of us and he probably wouldn't be too far wrong.*

She looked through the boat's open glass door and didn't see anyone inside. Lights were on, but it appeared to be empty. *That's strange,* she thought. *Chris told me there were only a few people living on their boats and this must be one, but why would someone leave their boat unlocked with the door to the cabin open and the lights on?* She remembered almost being shoved in the water by a young man as he was running up the gangway. *Maybe this is his boat, but I wonder why he had to leave in such a hurry.*

She and Rebel stepped inside the empty cabin of the boat. Rebel sniffed, growled, and then walked over to the side of the boat where a long bench was covered with upholstered pillows so it could be used for seating with storage underneath the seat. Rebel turned and looked up at Kelly expectantly. "Okay, I'll open it, but then we need to get out of here. Deal?"

She removed the two cream-colored pillows from the top of the bench seat and pulled up on the handle. When it swung open, she gasped and staggered back in shock. She couldn't believe what she'd just seen in the storage compartment. She was completely unnerved. Screwing up her courage, she looked inside again. Sure enough, there it was, a larger than life blown up nude photograph of Amber looking back at her with a large smile. She felt sick to her stomach. *Child, we never knew you*, she thought.

The interior of the storage bench contained some type of white powder residue and what looked like marijuana packaged in small baggies. Rebel continued to growl. *I've got to call Mike. Why would an erotic nude photograph of Amber be in here?*

Rebel suddenly barked aggressively and turned toward the open glass door of the boat. She followed his gaze and saw a large shadow immediately turn into the young man she'd seen a few minutes earlier on the gangway. Rebel stood between her and the man.

"What are you and that dog doing in here? You're trespassing. I'm tempted to call the sheriff."

Kelly took a long look at the young man in front of her. He had sea green eyes which were dilated and red-rimmed. Oily sandy hair, badly in need of being washed, hung down below his ears. From the looks of him he hadn't shaved for several days. "I wish you would call the sheriff, but first I'd like to know why you have a photograph of Amber."

"She was a friend of mine. How do you know her?" he asked.

"She was my godchild and she worked for me."

"Oh, yeah. She talked about you. You must be Kelly, the one who owns the coffee shop."

"I am and you are…"

"Name's Derek."

She could tell by his body mannerisms and blinking eyes that he was under the influence of drugs. She couldn't figure out why he would have Amber's picture and why Amber had never mentioned him if he was someone important enough to her that she'd allowed him to take a suggestive photograph of her in the nude.

Kelly looked past him and saw a small dinghy side-tied to his boat. Suddenly, it was like dominoes were tumbling one over the other in her brain. She knew who had killed Amber and why. It wasn't Chris after all; it was this young man standing in front of her. She put her hand in her pocket and secretly turned on the small recorder she'd put there earlier to record her expected conversation with Chris.

"You're the one who killed Amber, aren't you?" she blurted out.

He walked over to the drawer next to the pull-out dining table and took a pistol from it. When he turned back he said, "Keep that dog next to you. Looks like I'm going to have to do the same thing to you I did to Amber, but you know that, don't you?" He pointed the gun at them. "If you or the dog tries anything, I'll shoot you. I've got a silencer on this gun, so it won't make any noise. Just don't try anything."

She gave Rebel the stay command. "Why did you kill Amber? How did you meet her?"

"Might as well tell you since you won't be around to tell anyone else. I finished college in January and decided to take a few months off. My aunt said I could live on her boat for awhile. Gets lonesome out here all by myself. I like to read and one day when I was at the bookstore her mother owns I met her. We talked and I asked her to come out to the boat some time. She came that afternoon. Turns out she was hot, I mean really hot. I had her in bed in less than an hour. We had us quite a little affair going on for several weeks. Got her to pose in the nude for me while I took some photos. That was a couple of months ago.

"Yeah, I killed her. Dumb kid went and got herself knocked up. Thought I was the father. She came to my boat early one morning to tell me she was pregnant and asked me if I'd marry her. Like I'd marry anybody! Got some big plans I'm makin' and she wasn't a part of them. Gonna miss her."

"I'll bet you are. Who's your aunt?"

"Dottie Jones."

"You're Dottie's nephew?" she said, trying to reconcile this drugged-up young man with the warm, conservative woman she knew as Dottie.

"Yeah. My mom's her sister."

Of course Dottie would have found the blue ribbon on the gangway. It was probably just a few feet from his boat. Amber gave it to Derek and he probably lost it while he was stoned. It all makes sense.

"You almost knocked me into the water a little while ago. Where were you going so fast?"

"Met a man when I first came here that comes by once a week to sell me some things I need. His stuff is some of the best I've ever had and it keeps me stoked, if you know what I mean. Looked at my watch and realized I was going to miss him if I didn't hurry. Didn't have time for niceties. It was important that I see him so I could make a buy."

"I see. Derek, I can understand why you didn't want to marry Amber, but why did you have to kill her? Couldn't you just have left town? Was she in love with you?"

"Yeah, dumb little twit told me she loved me every time she came out here. Even though she knew I wasn't the kind to settle down with a wife and a baby, I think she had this fantasy that we'd be the perfect family. Kind of a thing where we'd all sing kumbaya. We did a lot of drugs when we first got together, but the last few weeks, she pretty much stopped. Guess it was because she knew she was pregnant. Probably heard that drugs aren't real good for a baby's health."

Drugs? Hot? Nude photos? Amber? This is a side of her I never saw and I hope her parents and everyone else never hear about it.

"Weren't you afraid someone would find out about you?"

"How could they? She sure wasn't going to tell people about me, her being so pure and the town sweetheart along with that boyfriend of hers. She told me about him and he sounded like a real wuss. He may have been the star of the football team, but she told me I was a lot more of a man than he was. Sex with Amber was good. I'm going to miss that."

"How did you kill her?"

"It was easy. She told me she was pregnant and was sure it was my baby. I told her how happy I was about it and that we should get married as soon as possible. I told her we needed to spend a little time together, if you know what I mean, and celebrate our baby. The rest was easy. While she was in bed, I told her I had to go to the head. I got one of my weights and put it behind my back. I kissed her and then hit her on the head with it as hard as I could. She didn't know anything from then on. I didn't want to shoot her because there'd be blood on the boat and my aunt is a real clean freak."

"So you put some weights in a burlap bag, tied the weighted bag to her body, and dropped her in the ocean."

"Yeah, that's pretty much what happened. I put her and the bag that was tied to her in the dinghy and covered her with a tarp. It was early and there's just a few people around here who live on their boats. I got in the dinghy and motored out a few hundred yards. I looked around and didn't see anyone. I lifted her out of the boat and eased her into the water on the seaward side of the dinghy, so no one could see what I was doing from shore. After that I came back to the boat, relaxed a little bit with some recreational stuff I have," he said, winking, "and fell asleep for the rest of the day. Next thing I knew someone was knocking on the door of the boat. It was the sheriff, asking if I knew anything about her death. Told him I didn't. That's about it. Think your time to be asking a bunch of dumb questions is about up. If you got any prayers to say or anything like that, might want to do it now. Think I'll do the dog first so he won't bark when I kill you."

Mike, I am so sorry. I should have kept my promise to Doc. I know who did it, but it sure isn't going to do any good. She bent down and scratched Rebel's ears, tears in her eyes. "You've been a good friend. So long. I love you"

CHAPTER TWENTY-THREE

Doc pulled in next to Kelly's car and turned to Mike. "Do you know which boat Chris owns?"

"Yes. I talked to all the live-aboards the night Amber was found. I remember he was at the end of the floating dock. We'll go down that first gangway. What's wrong?"

"Uh, Mike, I've never been on a dock before, much less a boat. You see, I'm terrified of being around water. I really don't feel good about it."

"Doc, look at it as a learning experience and that you'll probably be helping Kelly. Remember, you're the one who called me. Come on, we can't waste any more time. She's about ten minutes ahead of us as it is." He opened the door of Doc's truck as quietly as he could and took his gun from his holster. He noticed that Doc pulled a gun out from beneath his shirt. "Doc, are you authorized to carry that gun?"

"Yes. I've got a permit, but I've never done this before."

"Well just stay behind me and cover my back. Are you a good shot?"

"The best. Believe me, that's one thing you don't need to worry about."

Mike put up his hand. "Stop. Doc, did you hear that? It sounded like a dog bark."

Doc listened for a moment. "Don't hear a thing."

"I must be skittish, but it sounded like Rebel's bark, although I don't hear anything now. Come on."

The only sounds they heard were from the merrymaking at the yacht club and water gently lapping against the sides of the boats. The lights coming from Chris's boat, Avalon, glowed softly on the water. As they neared Chris's boat they heard music and Doc whispered, "I think he's playing Beethoven's Moonlight Sonata. If he wasn't a suspect, I'd be impressed."

"Well, don't be, because he's definitely a suspect in my book, although I don't hear any voices coming from his boat and you know how Kelly loves to talk."

When they reached the side of the boat, they looked in the window. Chris was sitting on his couch reading a book. There was no sign of Kelly or Rebel.

Mike knocked on the side of boat. A moment later Chris opened the glass sliding door at the rear of the boat and said, "Who is it?"

"Chris, it's Sheriff Mike. I need to talk to you a minute. Mind if I come on board? Have a friend with me. Okay?"

"Sure, Mike."

Mike looked over at Doc whose face was ashen. Doc whispered to Mike, "I can't do this."

"Yes, you can. You'll be fine. The boat's tied up and nothing's going to happen to you. Trust me."

"Mike, why do you have your gun drawn? Am I under arrest for something?" Chris said, laughing. "And your friend has a gun as well. What's going on?"

"Well, Chris. Why don't you tell us? Where are Kelly and Rebel?"

"I don't know. I haven't seen either one of them since this morning when I had breakfast at the coffee shop. Care to fill me in? I mean there must be some reason you're coming onto my boat with guns drawn."

Mike kept his gun in his hand. "Chris, you've become a prime suspect in Amber's case. Kelly told Doc she thought maybe you'd admit everything to her if she confronted you. He made her promise she wouldn't do it without me. She never called me and we have good reason to believe she's here. Her minivan is parked in its usual place in the lot."

"Wait a minute, Mike. I don't know what you're talking about. Amber was a student of mine and I saw her at the football games and with Brandon. That's it. She's never been on my boat and I've never seen her outside of class or on the football field. You're welcome to look around. What is it that makes you think I did it?"

"Later, Chris. Right now we've got to find Kelly. If she's not on your boat, she must be on someone else's." He turned to Doc. "Remember when I told you I thought I heard a dog bark. I'll bet it was Rebel." He turned back to Chris. "Who else lives on their boat down here?"

"I just remembered I saw Amber down here once. It looked like she was coming out of a boat one row over. I'd completely forgotten about it. At the time I thought it was odd, and that was the end of it."

"Do you know whose boat it is? Is someone living on it?"

"Yes, someone lives on it, but I don't know the guy's name. Think I heard that his aunt owned the boat and he was only going to stay on it for a few months. Do you think she could be there?"

"I don't know, but I'm going to find out. That was definitely the direction I heard the bark coming from. Doc, come on."

"Wait a minute, I'm coming too," Chris said. "If I'm a suspect, I'd like to clear my name. I don't own a gun, but with both of you packing, I probably don't need one."

Mike was back on the dock before Chris had finished speaking. Doc was right behind him, more than happy to get off of Chris's boat. Mike held his finger up to his lips indicating for them to be quiet. He looked over at the row of boats next to Chris's and he could see lights coming from the third boat down the dock. He motioned for them to follow him.

A few steps from the boat, Mike stopped and indicated that Chris and Doc were to stay there. He silently walked over to the boat and heard Kelly talking to Rebel. Instinctively, he jumped aboard. At the sound of Mike landing on his boat, Derek turned and fired a wild shot at him. Fortunately for Mike, the drugs Derek had used earlier affected his vision and the shot missed Mike by less than an inch.

"Attack, Rebel, attack," Kelly screamed at Rebel. In one blindingly fast movement Rebel leaped onto Derek, snarling and growling, biting the arm that held his gun. Derek fell to the floor, writhing in pain, his gun sliding out of his hand and clattering across the deck of the boat. Rebel stood on top of him, growling, his teeth inches from Derek's face. Doc and Chris jumped on board. Mike and Doc both pointed their guns at Derek.

"Kelly, get Rebel off of him."

"Rebel, stand down. Stand down, boy," she commanded. He walked over to her and lay down, panting. She rubbed his ears, "Good boy. You saved Mike's life and mine too."

"Get up," Mike said to Derek. "You've got some serious explaining to do."

"Mike, he killed Amber," Kelly blurted out. "I recorded it all. I know you told me not to buy that little miniature recorder when we saw it for sale on the Internet. You told me it was just a come-on, but I did it anyway. I hope it worked." She rewound the tape in the recorder and pressed the play button.

A second later, all of them heard, "You're the one who killed Amber..." She turned it off and smiled at Mike. "His full confession is on this recorder. Amber visited him the morning of the murder and told him she was pregnant. He pretended they needed to make love to celebrate their upcoming marriage and he hit her on the head with one of his weights. From there everything that happened was just like we've suspected. We just had the wrong man."

She turned to Chris. "I owe you a big apology. I was certain that you had killed Amber..."

Chris interrupted her. "Whatever made you think that? My sister was murdered and I still have nightmares about it. That's why I don't own a gun. I'm the type that takes spiders outside and lets them go rather than kill them. I'd be the last person to kill anything. I can't believe you thought I was the killer. I felt like we were friends. I noticed you got kind of funny when you saw the free weights on my boat and I couldn't figure out why."

"Think about it, Chris," Kelly said. "You're a good looking man, a man a young woman might have fantasies about. You live on your boat. You row your boat every morning and you knew Amber. She was drowned in the bay. Only someone who had a boat or access to a boat could have taken her out into the bay and dumped her body overboard. There aren't many people who live on their boats here at the marina, so you were a natural suspect. I pretty much eliminated the other suspects, but I couldn't eliminate you."

"Wait a minute, Kelly," Mike said. "What do you mean 'you eliminated them? I think once again you've forgotten that I'm the sheriff of this county and this case is not only in my jurisdiction, but officially it's my case, not yours."

"You're absolutely right. I just know how busy you are and I wanted to help you."

"You helped all right. You solved the case, but you almost got both you and Rebel killed in the process. Do me a favor and don't try to help me with any more cases. Deal?"

"Deal," she said, mentally crossing her fingers.

"I heard Kelly call you Derek. Derek, you're under arrest for the murder of Amber Cook. I'm going to read you your Miranda rights and then we're going to take a little trip to the county jail. You'll be arraigned and then a trial date will be set. Don't know if you have any money, but the judges in this county don't look too kindly on letting accused murderers out on bail, so even if you do have some money, don't think that will happen. Doc, keep him covered while I get the Miranda card out of my wallet." He read Derek his rights and then called his deputy to come down to the marina. He told his deputy he didn't have his car and he had a prisoner in custody that needed to be transported to the county jail.

"Kelly, I think it's time for you and Rebel to go home. I'll be along when I finish this up. Doc, thanks for following your gut instinct and calling me when Kelly promised you she wouldn't visit Chris without me." He looked over at Kelly who had a very contrite look on her face.

"Chris, you can go back to your boat and listen to the rest of the sonata. Sorry I had to bother you, but I'm sure after you've had a chance to think about it, you'll realize you were a very viable suspect. I'm glad it wasn't you." Mike turned to Doc, "Derek's going to walk up the gangway and into the parking lot where my deputy's car should be waiting. I'll be right behind him with my gun on him and I'd like you to follow us in case he has any last minute grandiose ideas like jumping into the ocean and swimming to safety. If he makes a move, shoot him."

"It would be my pleasure," Doc said.

The three of them made their way up the gangway where the red and blue lights on top of the deputy's car were blinking in the parking lot.

Kelly turned to Rebel and said, "Well, Rebel, that was a little more exciting than I'd planned. Good boy. Think we need to get home and give you some treats, however, I'm not sure what the proper food is to give a dog that has just saved my life."

He let out a woof, wagged his tail, and followed her up the gangway.

CHAPTER TWENTY-FOUR

The graduates filed into the school auditorium, black caps and gowns on, proud looks on both their faces and the faces of their family members. Mike squeezed Kelly's hand knowing how hard it must be for her not to see her goddaughter graduate. Amber's parents, Ginger and Bob, had chosen not to attend the graduation. Their loss was still too fresh for them to sit through the graduation ceremony. The town had been full of rumors the last two days, and as usual, some were right and some weren't. All that was really known was that Dottie's nephew had been arrested on her boat and charged with murdering Amber.

Dr. Ricketts, the school principal, walked up to the podium. The faculty members were seated behind him. He spoke for a few moments and then began calling out the names of the graduating seniors. After their name had been called, the students walked across the stage and Dr. Ricketts' secretary handed them their rolled diploma tied with a blue ribbon. The high school in Cedar Bay wasn't a large one and it didn't take long to call the names of the one hundred twenty-six graduates. After the last diploma had been given out, Dr. Ricketts again stepped to the podium.

"Today it is my distinct pleasure to introduce Brandon Black who will deliver the valedictorian address. I've known Brandon since he came to Cedar Bay High School as a freshman. While his performance as a quarterback has already become legendary, I want everyone here to know that his academic accomplishments are equally legendary. It is rare to have a student graduate with a perfect 4.0 average, but Brandon was able to do that. He is a role model for every current student as well as future students, and although he will be missed, all of us will be following his next challenge, playing football for Oregon State on a full scholarship. What most people don't know is that not only was he awarded a football scholarship, if he had chosen not to play for Oregon State, the university also offered him a full academic scholarship. To say this school is proud of his achievements would be the understatement of the year. Ladies and gentlemen, I can think of no one more deserving to deliver the valedictorian address than Brandon Black."

The applause was thunderous as Brandon stepped onto the stage. He waited a moment for the crowd to become quiet and then began. A pin drop silence settled over the audience as everyone prepared to listen to what he was going to say. The rapt audience knew about the events of the last two weeks, or at least most of those events.

"Thank you ladies and gentlemen and fellow graduates. I would be remiss if I didn't dedicate this address to a young woman we all loved and looked up to – Amber Cook. As I'm sure you know, she was very close to me and I will miss her every day for the rest of my life. I honestly believe she's looking down on us at this moment, wanting us to remember her, but most of all, wanting us to move on with our lives."

Kelly leaned over and whispered to Mike. "I am so glad that Brandon doesn't know the truth about Amber."

"Me too," he said.

Sniffles were heard throughout the auditorium and many people in the audience reached into their pocket or purse to get a Kleenex or handkerchief. All of them knew how hard this must be for Brandon.

He continued, "What the events of the last two weeks have taught me is how precious every moment of our lives is. We never know when tragedy or unforeseen events will change our lives. The coming years will bring tremendous changes to each of the lives of the graduates who are here today. Some of us are going to college, some of us are starting careers, and some of us are getting married and beginning our families. Changes. Some will be good, some won't. We must cherish the good moments and find something good in the bad moments. Only by doing that can we live our lives fully. Only by doing that, cherishing each moment, can we keep some type of control over our lives.

"I hope when we return for our ten year reunion, each one of you will come up to me and say, "Brandon, there were times I didn't think I could go on, times when I hated my life, times when I was so down I didn't think I could ever get up again, but I remembered the words you said at our graduation, 'cherish the moment,' and I knew I could get through it. My friends and fellow graduates, cherishing the moment and fully living it, is far more important than the score on a football scoreboard or the results of an exam. If you remember nothing from this graduation day, but 'cherish the moment,' all the pain I've been through these last few days will be worth it. So I say to you, believe in yourself and cherish the moment! Thank you."

As he walked off the stage, the audience rose as one, clapping and yelling. In seconds the auditorium erupted into a chant, "Brandon, Brandon." In that seminal moment, the little town of Cedar Bay healed as they cherished one of their own.

Dr. Ricketts stepped back to the podium and spent five minutes to no avail trying to quiet the crowd. When it became clear that the crowd was never going to become quiet, he yelled, "Ladies and gentlemen, that concludes our graduation ceremony. Graduates, you may toss your caps in the air and begin your new lives."

Caps filled the air above the heads of the graduates. The seniors of Cedar Bay High School were now alumni, fully ready to face and take on the world.

*****

"Mike, wasn't that about the best graduation ceremony you've ever attended? I feel cleansed, like this horrible thing is over and because of Brandon, I really had the sense that everyone else did too. You mentioned that you thought Derek's attorney would cut a deal with the prosecutor and plead guilty to a lesser charge so there wouldn't be a trial. I hope he does. I really don't want anyone to know the truth about Amber, particularly Brandon, Ginger, and Bob."

"I have a feeling he will. The evidence against him is pretty solid and there's a good chance the jury would find him guilty and give him the death penalty. Not that it wouldn't be fitting in his case. Anyway, Brandon's an amazing young man. I don't know many people who could do what he did this afternoon. I imagine we'll hear a lot about him in the future, and given his speech today, I'm sure it will all be positive."

"Mike, I want to apologize again about the Chris and Derek thing. I was wrong. I should have called you. I guess you didn't even need to come here and stay at my house to protect me, although I'm glad you did. Obviously at that time Derek wasn't a threat to me, nor was Chris."

"Well, Kelly," he said standing up and walking over to where she was seated on the deck, looking out at the bay. "It made something perfectly clear to me. I realized I couldn't stand for anything to happen to you. I may not have shown it, but I don't think I've ever been so scared in my life." He got down on one knee. "I know it's kind of hokey, but would you marry me?" He took a small box out of the pocket of his pants and held it up to her. She opened it. Inside was a beautiful emerald cut diamond. "Kelly, if you agree to marry me I don't think Julia or Cash would object if I moved in permanently. I called both of them to ask their permission to marry you and they seemed absolutely fine with it. Matter of fact, they were kind of enthusiastic, so what do you say?"

"Oh Mike. It's beautiful and the answer is, yes, yes, yes." He slipped the ring on her finger and stood up, pulling her to him.

"I think I know an even better way to celebrate than kissing on the deck. Come on," he said.

She smiled and followed Mike into the house. Rebel sensed that this would be a good time for him to stay on the deck. He knew Mike would protect her and he could rest for a little while.

RECIPES

JANE'S SAUSAGE CASSEROLE

12 slices of sourdough bread, cut into 2" cubes
1 ½ pounds Jimmy Dean mild sausage
1 7 ounce can of chopped green chilies
3 cups cheddar cheese, grated
2 ½ cups milk
4 eggs
1 can golden mushroom soup mixed with ¼ cup milk (to be prepared next day)
1 teaspoon dry mustard
Salt and pepper to taste

Grease a 9 x 13 Pyrex glass dish and place the bread in the bottom of it. Brown and drain the sausage. Add chilies, cheese, and sausage to the bread. Stir lightly. Mix eggs, milk, mustard, salt, and pepper together and pour over the mixture in the glass dish. Cover with saran wrap and refrigerate overnight.

The next day, remove the dish from refrigerator and preheat the oven to 325 degrees. Prepare mushroom mixture and pour it over casserole.

Bake for 1 hour and 15 minutes, uncovered. Let stand 10 minutes before serving. Don't overbake! It will firm up during the 10 minute cooling time. Enjoy!

DECADENT BACON CHOCOLATE-CHIP COOKIES

2 ½ cups flour
2 eggs
1 teaspoon baking soda
¼ teaspoon baking powder
¾ teaspoon salt
1 cup unsalted butter, softened
¾ cup granulated sugar
¾ cup packed light brown sugar
1 teaspoon vanilla extract
12 ounces chocolate chips
12 ounces bacon

Preheat oven to 375 degrees.

Fry the bacon and drain it on a paper towel. When the bacon is cool, break it into small pieces or put the pieces in a large plastic bag and use a rolling pin to break them up.

Combine the flour, baking soda, baking powder, and salt into a small bowl. Mix the butter, sugars, and vanilla until well combined. Add the eggs, one at a time, beating well after each. Gradually beat in the flour mixture. When combined, stir in the chocolate chips and bacon pieces. Drop rounded teaspoons of the cookie dough onto parchment lined cookie sheets. Bake in the oven for 9 to 11 minutes or until golden brown. Let stand for 2 minutes and remove to a wire rack to cool completely.Enjoy!

MAMA DEE'S BARBECUED BRISKET

5-6 pound brisket
3 ounces liquid smoke
5 tablespoon worcestershire sauce
Onion salt
Salt and pepper

Place the brisket in a glass baking dish. Add the liquid smoke, 3 tablespoons of worcestershire sauce, and seasonings. Cover with tin foil and refrigerate overnight.

Preheat the oven to 275 degrees. When ready to bake, drain off the seasonings. Sprinkle with the remaining Worcestershire sauce, salt, and pepper. Cover with foil and bake for 5 hours. Let cool. Can be made up to a day in advance. Sauce can be made in advance as well. (I often double the sauce recipe to keep a good barbecue sauce on hand.)

BARBECUE SAUCE

1 cup catsup
½ cup lemon juice
1 cup water
½ cup worcestershire sauce
1 teaspoon each of chili powder, salt, and celery seed.

Bring all to a boil and simmer until thickened.

One hour before serving, slice the brisket and pour some of the sauce between and on top of the slices. Bake one more hour at 275. Serve with the sauce on the side.

Leftovers are great slightly warmed and in sandwiches. Enjoy!

START MY DAY APPLE STUFFED FRENCH TOAST

12 slices Italian bread
½ cup butter, cubed
1 cup packed light brown sugar
2 tablespoons light corn syrup
2 large tart apples, peeled and thinly sliced
1 cup chopped pecans
6 eggs
1 ½ cups milk
1 ½ teaspoons ground cinnamon
¼ teaspoon ground nutmeg
¼ teaspoon salt
1 teaspoon vanilla extract

In a small saucepan combine the brown sugar, butter, and corn syrup. Cook over medium heat until thickened, stirring occasionally. Pour mixture into a greased 9 x 13 baking dish. Top with half of the pecans, a single layer of bread, and the other half of the pecans. Arrange the apples and remaining bread over the top.

In a large bowl whisk the eggs, milk, cinnamon, nutmeg, salt, and vanilla together. Pour over the bread. Cover with plastic wrap and refrigerate overnight.

When ready to bake, preheat the oven to 350 degrees. Bake uncovered for 35 – 40 minutes or until lightly browned. Let stand for five minutes and invert. While baking, make sauce.

CARAMEL SAUCE

½ cup light brown sugar
¼ cup unsalted butter, cubed
1 tablespoon light corn syrup

Combine the sauce ingredients and stir over medium heat until thickened. Serve with the French toast. Enjoy!

KELLY'S CHEESECAKE

CRUST
¼ cup sugar
6 tablespoons melted butter
1 ¼ cups chocolate wafers, crushed (a food processor works well for this)
Combine and press into 8" spring form pan with removable bottom.

FILLING
½ cup heavy cream
24 oz. cream cheese
4 eggs

1 cup granulated sugar
1 teaspoon vanilla extract

Preheat oven to 350 degrees. When the cream cheese, eggs, and cream are at room temperature, addthe sugar and vanilla, mixing until there are no lumps of cream cheese. Pour into the crust and bake for approximately 70 minutes or when the center no longer jiggles. Let cool and refrigerate overnight.

TOPPING

1 jar hot fudge topping
1 jar caramel topping
1 cup chopped pecans (optional)

Spoon the hot fudge around the border of the cheesecake. Make an interior circle with the caramel topping. If using pecans, scatter them over the top. Refrigerate until served. When ready to serve, remove sides of spring form pan.

ABOUT THE AUTHOR

Dianne lives in Huntington Beach, California with her husband Tom, a former California State Senator, and is a frequent contributor to the Huffington Post. Her other award winning books include:

Blue Coyote Motel
Coyote in Provence
Cornered Coyote

Tea Party Teddy
Tea Party Teddy's Legacy

Website: www.dianneharman.com
Email: dianne@dianneharman.com

Gloucester Library
P.O. Box 2380
Gloucester, VA 23061

Made in the USA
Charleston, SC
09 December 2014